Joanna's Miracle

Joanna's Miracle

by William H. Armstrong

Broadman Press
Nashville, Tennessee

Dewey Decimal Classification: F

Subject Heading: JESUS CHRIST—MIRACLES—FICTION

Library of Congress Catalog Card Number: 77-089708

Printed in the United States of America

Contents

Other Books by William H. Armstrong:

Animal Tales
Barefoot in the Grass: the Story of Grandma Moses
87 Ways to Help Your Child in School
Hadassah: Esther, the Orphan Queen
My Animals
Peoples of the Ancient World
Sounder
Sour Land
Study Is Hard Work
Study Tips
The Education of Abraham Lincoln
The MacLeod Place
The Mills of God
Through Troubled Waters
Tools of Thinking
Word Power in Five Easy Lessons

All Scripture verses are taken from the Revised Standard Version of the Bible.

"But there are also many other things which Jesus did; were every one of them to be written, I suppose that the world itself could not contain the books."

John 21:25

"For everything there is a season . . . . a time to weep, and a time to laugh; a time to mourn, and a time to dance."

Ecclesiastes 3:1, 4

"God—the pathway of his progress is hard to find. And yet it shines out through the gloom in the dark chance of human life. Effortless and calm—he works his perfect will."

Aeschylus

Chapter One

"My shepherd is coming, and he sings as he comes, with many shekels in his girdle from selling his lambs, and good news for Joanna." The girl raised herself from the milk stool and looked over the courtyard toward the north, where the road followed the spine of the rugged hill country of Palestine. The girl who spoke was Martha, the older of the two daughters of Judith. Judith was a hill woman who sat as though enchanted by the spat-spat of goat's milk into a clay bowl as she rhythmically stripped the last few drops of milk and moved to another goat, calling each by name.

"If he's singing, that means he brings good news for me, and I'll be happier to see him than Martha will"— this from a girl about fourteen who sat on the steps that led from the courtyard to the living quarters above the animal yard.

"Have no mind for his singing." The mother stopped her rhythm for an instant. "He sings all the time. Martha, get back to your milking. I'll have little help from you after your Benjamin enters the gate. And Joanna, don't let that pet lamb go up the steps. It tries

9

to go straight for the barley mortar every time I open the door."

Joanna did not answer her mother. She moved the lamb back gently to the step below her and cradled its head in her lap, stroking its back and speaking softly. "You can run away from me when you are frisky on the way to pasture; but soon I will be able to catch you, if Benjamin brings me word."

"The bowl is ready, and don't fall over that lamb and spill it," the woman said as she raised herself and stood waiting in the middle of the animals.

Now Joanna pushed the lamb aside and stood up. One arm was concealed inside her robe. One foot made a sharp clop sound as she descended the steps. A thick block of wood with a sandal strap showed below the hem of her garment. She walked among the animals with an almost stalklike, swinging limp. The rim of the milk bowl she pressed into her side, grasping the outer edge with the one arm that showed outside her robe.

"You could use two hands if . . ." but the mother did not finish. The voice of Martha's shepherd boy, Benjamin, called "Hallo" as he swung the gate wide and entered.

Joanna's part of the milking was to carry in the milk, strain it into the settling bowls, and then wash the wide-mouthed ones from which she poured the milk. She couldn't actually milk the goats, for goats bear twins and give down their milk from both sides of their udders at the same time. And Joanna had only one good hand. Hidden under her robe she carried a lifeless, stiff, and withered arm. And if only one side of

a goat's udder is milked, it kicks and walks away.
That's why the rare single-born goat or lamb learns
quickly to alternate often and fast between both sides
of the udder.

"Come up into the quarters," Martha said to Benjamin. "Joanna wants to hear of your journey."

"Are you sure the gate is latched?" the mother asked
as she walked in front of Martha and Benjamin up the
steps where Joanna had disappeared. The clop-clop-
clop of her heavy wooden sandal had been replaced by
the intermittent bleating of the pet lamb from his
perch on the top step.

When they were seated around the brazier where a
low fire smoldered in the middle of the room, Benjamin
began to speak. But Joanna sat a little back from the
circle, leaning forward, her dark eyes flashing with
questions that could not escape Benjamin. He turned
his eyes down to gaze upon the red glow of the dung fire
and traced aimlessly with his finger in the dirt floor.

"I went as far north as Nain," he said quietly, "but
there I learned that it was useless to go farther. He has
gone out of the province of Herod, north by Galilee and
across the Jordan toward Caesarea Philippi, for Herod
had sent word that he wanted to see him. The people in
Nain said that the Pharisees had reported to Herod
that Jesus had healed a man with a withered hand on
the sabbath day. Herod did not care anything about
the observance of the sabbath, but he thought that
Jesus might be John the Baptist raised from the dead. I
guess Herod felt guilty because he had been tricked by
Herodias, his wicked wife, into executing John."

"But do you not think Jesus might come back and

pass this way? It is the time of the Passover, and he might be going to Jerusalem." As Joanna spoke, her voice quivered.

"No. But he is going to Jerusalem. He sent word back to Herod, and this is exactly what the people of Nain told me Jesus said: 'Go and tell that sly old fox that I will continue healing all manner of diseases and casting out devils. And if he wants to see me it'll be in Jerusalem.' So I guess he is definitely going to the Passover. But Herod won't go to Jerusalem. A caravan driver I met on the way home says that Pilate, the Roman governor, took Herod's palace in Jerusalem, and that they're not on speaking terms. Pilate hates Herod because he's a troublemaker."

"You see, Mother?" Joanna spoke with a touch of bitterness in her voice. "I could have gone to Nain. He healed a man with a withered hand."

"How could you have gone to Nain? We have no donkey; it's three days' walking from here for somebody not crippled. You would have been hobbling on the road a week. And all kinds of things could have happened. You're a girl now, no longer a child; and the lust of the highwaymen cares little between the fit and the unfit."

"But he did much more than heal the man with the withered hand," Benjamin said, interrupting the hollow, hopeless voice of the woman.

"I'll light the lamp before you continue." Martha spoke quietly as she put her hand on Benjamin's shoulder and started to rise.

"No. There's light enough from the fire," the woman said. "We must save the little oil we have."

"Mother, Mother," Martha said as she sighed heavily and sank back on the mat beside Benjamin.

"I heard so much." Benjamin started again. "I remember some of the places, but I couldn't keep it all straight. The people always seemed so excited and talked so fast—running one story upon another."

"Could the man with the withered hand raise it above his head after he was healed? Could he pick up a bowl or a shepherd's crook?" Joanna asked, her voice rising and hurrying one word after another.

"I didn't hear what he did, but it must have been something. The Pharisees saw enough, or they wouldn't have gone running to Herod. They'd have to know for sure.

"But right in the village of Nain there was this woman—a widow, too—and I tried to find her, but she was out working or driving her flock. An old man told me, 'Her boy had been down with sleeping sickness. He was shrunk away to nothing and had been in a deep sleep. Some said he was dead. Well, Jesus took hold of his limp hand; and the boy awoke out of it and began to speak. He got better from that day on.' That's how the old man told it. But I wanted to talk to the mother, too."

"That must have been last year, when we heard the sleeping sickness was going around," Martha said.

"And that's about the time we first heard that the miracle worker was in the north country. I should have gone right then."

"And brought sleeping sickness back to the hill country?" Judith broke in upon Joanna. "Besides, it was only several months ago that we first heard, and then there were different stories. Some said he was just another fake faith healer or fiery zealot who, like Rosh bar-Judas of Galilee, would get a lot of people killed."

"Well, there are still different stories; and some people say when you ask them about him, 'Don't waste my time! Wild stories!' A caravan driver laughed and said, 'A carpenter gone berserk. I've seen these sand-dune preachers and healers from the bazaars of Palmyra to the temple colonnades in Egypt. They come out of the desert with their visions. I've been in and out of the deserts for a long time, but I have no visions to report except some robber lurking in the way to rob me of my goods.' "

Benjamin continued. "Three different people—I guess they were doubters—told me that 'this Jesus,' as they called him, wasn't even believed by his own people. When he tried to speak in the synagogue at Nazareth, his hometown, they were offended that one trained as a carpenter, not as a rabbi, should think he could teach them. So they threw him out. And as he was leaving he said, 'No prophet is believed in his own country. He is honored elsewhere, but not ever among his own people or by his own kinfolk.' And he left there and went down to Capernaum to preach."

"What'd he preach about? Like John the Baptist—repent, repent?" Judith asked with a hint of boredom in her voice. There was also an intonation of: *Haven't we had about enough? We are only hill women who have to get up with the dawn and drag through another day of scratching a meager existence out of the bony, resisting hills of Israel.*

"But I want to hear more about his healing," Joanna

insisted, flashing her dark eyes and leaning forward into the narrowing circle of the fire's diminishing glow.

"Yes," Martha added as she went to the corner and picked up a small wooden scoop of dung chips, feeding them to the fire. She said in a firm but not at all disrespectful way, "Let Benjamin tell it the way he wants, Mother. He went to all the trouble to find out for Joanna."

"But he was going anyway, wasn't he, taking his lambs to sell for the Passover sacrifice at the synagogue in Nain?"

"And remember you said I would lose half of them to wild animals or they would get lost in the thicket on the way? Well, I didn't lose a single one. They followed the old lead goat as though she was the mother of them all." The boy squeezed Martha's hand as he spoke. It was his way of saying: *Judith will be a hard mother-in-law; but don't you worry, Martha. I love you.*

"And all three nights along the way I found sheep-folds, and the shepherds who owned them welcomed me to use them for a night. But I didn't sell a single lamb to the priest at Nain. I got a better price selling them from house to house—mostly fishermen, you know. The price was good, too, because the Romans at Tiberias buy a lot to feed the soldiers there. And some-times drive off half a flock and don't pay, one man said. But I'm not sure he was telling the truth; he was very bitter about things. When I asked him if he knew anything about the Man from Nazareth, he said, 'Wild stories! Gossip! I've heard the wild stories, but I keep the Law and my mouth shut. There's too much trouble being stirred up in the land.' Anyway, he bought the old lead goat. I didn't much want him to have her, but the people there are mainly fishermen or wine growers; so I didn't have any other offers. I hope he will be good to her. Now I'll begin to tame a leader for next year."

Small flames, alternating blue and gold, danced back and forth on the surface of the dung chips. Sometimes they leaped from one chip to another or spurted spearlike toward one or another of the figures around the fire. They rose and fell, their patterns dispelling here and there the ringed darkness behind the four people. They played their light upon one object or another: the wide footbath bowl just inside the doorway; a vertical loom standing against the wall near the mother's bed; the sleeping mats of the girls; the milk bowls; a mortar and pestle; two tall water jars; a graining sieve hung from a beam; and a flat olive-oil lamp, unlit, on the stool where Martha had placed it when the mother had forbidden its lighting.

There had been a long quiet after Benjamin finished telling about the business part of his trip north. The three young people gazed at the fire; the mother nodded, lifted her heavy eyelids, stirred, then let them droop again.

Benjamin wanted to tell what he had heard about the preaching of the Man from Nazareth. He wanted to tell Martha especially. And he wanted to tell Joanna about how Jesus had healed the Roman captain's friend, without even going near him, and how mad the incident had made the priest in Capernaum. He thought, though, that he had better go now. He would drive his flock with theirs tomorrow; and in the high pasture, with Judith left below in the fields, he could tell Martha and Joanna.

But now the quiet was suddenly broken. Judith no longer nodded. She sat bolt-upright.

"Mother." Joanna had spoken quietly. "I could go to Jerusalem and find Jesus there. It's three days until Passover, and Jerusalem is only a two days' journey."

"But for you it would be three days or more," the woman snapped. "For a girl, you know how dangerous the roads are, especially with all the crowds going for the Passover."

"I could fall in with some good people. I've watched them passing on the road below the pastures for several days already, and there are more and more each day. Watching them, I wondered if we would all ever go again like we did when I was ten, before Father died."

"Then we had a donkey for you to ride. Then we had Jonas, your father, to take care of us." Now the woman's voice turned from reason to scorn. "Jerusalem killed my Jonas. Jerusalem took away my life, all that I had. Jerusalem is sorrow for me—not joy. Could I go into Jerusalem singing the hymns of peace as I go? I can only weep.

"Jonas should never have listened to Rosh bar-Judas. I remember his very words. He sat right here and persuaded Jonas. 'That Pilate and his cutthroat soldiers must be driven out,' he said. 'He has defiled the city and the Temple. And now he plans to take the money from the Temple treasury and build an aqueduct to bring water from the upper springs into Jerusalem. For a thousand years, since David, people have had plenty of water from the springs of Gihon and the pool of Siloam and the pool of Bethesda.'

"And Rosh bar-Judas talked on and on. He stirred up your father. I begged Jonas not to go. I told him they'd all end up the way Rosh's older brother, Judas of Galilee, did, when they revolted up there. They'd be hanged on the trees that lined the road just like the agitators in Galilee. But Jonas listened to Rosh bar-Judas. 'I have to go,' he said. 'I have to go.' Jonas was a deeply spiritual man. But he was impaled on a stake by Pilate's soldiers along with Rosh bar-Judas and the rest. So Jerusalem has no meaning for me but sorrow."

"But Jesus will never come this way now because of Herod. And I could find the house in the Street of the Dung Gate where Rhoda lives in the lodging house of your cousin Rebecca Mark."

"Don't speak to me of that heartless Rebecca Mark. She could have gone and claimed Jonas' body the day before the sabbath and given her own kin a decent burial. She didn't. I'd never speak to her if I went to Jerusalem a hundred times. And you won't either."

"I could find Rhoda. She was Martha's friend, and mine, before she left to live in Jerusalem."

"She didn't go to live in the city. Why use nice words for that tramp? She ran away when her hardworking parents, Aaron and Riuka, betrothed her to Simon, James of Sela's son. They had her dowry ready. The kin had been invited. She put Aaron and Riuka to shame. Simon is a good man. He's lucky that she ran away. He married well, and his flocks increase each year.

"No, child, you'll have nothing to do with that Rhoda. She might be a servant in Rebecca Mark's lodging house, and she might not. More likely she's roaming the Street of the Bazaars or loitering at the Gate of the Wicked, wearing a bright red girdle and laughing outside, but grieving inside for the life she's lost. Her dowry ready . . ."

"Don't be so cruel, Mother," Martha interrupted. She knew how many times her mother had reminded Benjamin that she'd have no dowry for her girls. And Benjamin was always embarrassed. He wanted no dowry. And he and Martha would already be married if Martha's father hadn't been killed in the revolt. Always her mother said, "After the planting . . . after the lambing . . . after the harvest gathering . . ." But Martha and Benjamin knew that one day they would marry.

Joanna now sat in silence. Martha watched her lips, drawn and quivering. Even in the dim light of the fire she could see the diamond-point of tears streaming down Joanna's sun-brown cheeks.

How beautiful her sister was, with her dark hair falling over her shoulders and her bright eyes made brighter by her tears. Her robe spread to hide her crippled left side.

Chapter Two

Martha pitied her mother's bitterness. Her father's death had begun it. Her mother was always repeating the story. And for the past couple of years, with Joanna passing childhood, Martha had come to feel that her mother was growing to think of Joanna as a burden. Often when the two of them were alone, with Joanna out of hearing, her mother would go over the painful details of Joanna's birth.

"She was born in the field, earlier than I thought," her mother would begin. "No time to get to the house and send for Marian, the midwife. Your father spread his tunic on the earth beside a thornbush, the only shade from the scorching sun. You've seen him in the sheepfold, delivering a lamb born backward, calling to one of us to hold onto the ewe while he braced his heels in the earth. He would pull and pull until the ewe, and whoever was trying to hold her, were dragged along, leaving a bloody path smeared upon the earth behind them. There was no one to hold me, so I held onto the thornbush. My hands bled; my screams became sobs and whimpers. Darkness at last overtook me.

"When I came to I could see the terror in your father's eyes. He held the crying baby in his arms, wrapped in my turban. I had hoped for a son to help your father in the fields. But the look in his eyes was more than disappointment.

" 'You have another beautiful daughter,' he said. 'She has a twisted foot, only a little. I am a poor midwife, I guess. It'll straighten out—like fixed joints in newborn lambs. Sometimes the joints of their front legs are bent and they walk on their knees for a day or two. We'll call her Beulah, beautiful daughter,' your father said. But when I held her and looked at half a child, rosy and pink, and the other wrinkled and pale, with a foot bent straight across and under, I cried out, 'We will call her Shamir, born under a thornbush.'

"Then your father shamed me and said, 'We'll call her Judith, lovely like her mother.' How strange it was. Instead of hurrying from the fields to cleanse the child in a salt-bath and wrap it in swaddling bands, I gave it suck, and we sat there arguing over names. 'I wanted a son for you,' I said. 'We'll call her Joanna, daughter of Jonas.'

"And all the time I kept my eyes on you, climbing among the rocks, outrunning the lambs. My heart filled up with gall, for I knew she never would."

Martha had been watching Joanna's tears. She wished her mother would not continue. Surely in all her bitterness there was yet a lot of love.

"They had her dowry ready," the mother repeated, and now her talk grew loud. "Fall in with good people on the way, you say? It's easier to fall in with bad people. There are more of them. Is it for the Passover

that many go? They go for a meat feast—a carnival, a
parade for their new Passover robes and mantles. They
chant their chants—'God delivered us; God will come
again.' And when it's over they straggle home to find
half their flock missing—stolen or devoured. Then they
lament, 'God is not kind to me.'

"Once I, too, dreamed of new Passover robes and
mantles. Not for me—for you.

"That's what Rosh bar-Judas said to my Jonas.
'We're with the good people. They have sent me word.
They need our help this once only. A lot from Galilee
have already gone. We're gathering at Anathoth. More
are coming from the hills. We'll begin at the Serpent's
Pool under cover of darkness, and Pilate's aqueduct
will lay in heaps of stone—right up to the city wall.' "

"Mother," Martha said in a half-whisper, "please
don't go on so, with Benjamin here. Joanna only men-
tioned going to Jerusalem to find the great healer from
Nazareth. If she cannot go to Jerusalem, perhaps she
could wait until the Passover is over, go down across
the Jordan, and look for him along the East Road as he
makes his way back to Galilee. They say the region is
safe; soldiers patrol all the roads of the Decapolis."

"That would be worse! Since when do Rome's
scavengers of lust give protection to a girl?"

Now Joanna began to sob with the spastic sob of a
child who is innocent before a relentless accuser, help-
less before a world that seems to have no understanding and desires none.

"Next year we'll inquire before I drive my lambs to
market, and you can go with me." Benjamin had sat
quietly for a long time. "Or if the wool buyer doesn't

come after the shearing, we might go between shearing and barley harvest."

"It'll be the same." Joanna choked between her sobbing. "I wanted to go before, when we first heard that he was real. I wanted to go when you were going to Nain. But always I hear 'Wait till we're sure he is not another fake and pretender, like so many we've heard about before.'"

"I promise you we'll go." Martha reached over and touched her sister's good hand.

"And who knows," Benjamin said softly, "the Man from Nazareth might yet come into the hill country. With Herod and his brother Philip fighting over Philip's wife, and Pilate not liking Herod's stirring up trouble among the people, old Herod might not be around much longer for the Man of Nazareth to fear. I think Jesus will be here a long time after Herod's gone. If it was urgent, I'd leave everything and go with you across the river to wait for him to come back from the Passover. But my father is too old to go about the shearing of the flock alone, and the ticks are already crawling in the sun."

"And you must help us, too, I hope," the mother said. "The roaming shearers say what portion of the wool they'll take for labor, but they always steal more." Now she lapsed into a quiet monologue, talking to herself. "I always wanted my girls to have a fine linen garment. But here in the hills, with Jonas gone, we're doomed to wear goat's hair. A robe of pure linen for each—wide sleeves in Joanna's, trimmed bright, with a matching girdle. Long, too, it would be, just skirt the ground almost, and a border, too. If not linen instead of goat's hair, then wool from lamb's fleece. But always we have to sell the wool to buy salt.

"It's time for sleep," she said abruptly as if coming from a dream. "Martha, don't forget to turn the foot bowl over the fire after Benjamin finds his way. Come for the shearing soon," she said, but did not address the boy by name.

As soon as the door latch rattled in its keeper, there came a loud bleating from the yard below. Now Joanna got up and followed Martha and Benjamin to the door.

"You'll have to calm that pesky lamb," her sister said. Joanna clop-clopped down two steps. She took the lamb, which had already run halfway to meet her, in her arms and sat down on the steps. Martha and Benjamin sat on the step behind her. The moon was high; it ran a thin black rim around the wall in the animal yard. And now with Joanna running her hand through its moist fleece, the lamb was quiet. The rhythmic chewing of the animals' cuds and the low mournful night cooing of a dove, awakened by the bleating of the lamb, only pronounced the living silence that lay upon the earth.

The points of hills alternated gray and gold under the moon; the scattered yew trees marked the lines of fields, keeping their darkness of the day, defying the moon.

"Your mother asked me what I heard his preaching was like, but I never got a chance to answer her. I wanted to. He tells stories that people can understand. He talks about planting and gathering in, the seasons and flowers, trees and thorns, shepherds and stray sheep. He makes poor people feel good. He says not to

worry too much about this world. I remember a couple
of beautiful stories that a beggar told me outside the
gate at Nain.

"The beggar's exact words were: 'Don't be too anxious
about what you have to eat and drink or what you
wear. Look at the birds that fly across the heavens,
singing all day. They don't sow, and they don't worry
about harvesttime. They don't gather in and store up
in granaries and barns. But God feeds them. And are
not you of much more value than they are?

" 'Think of the lilies of the field, how they grow. They
toil not; neither do they spin. But not even Solomon in
all his royal robes was arrayed as one of these. If God
clothes the grass of the field, which grows for such a
short time until it is cut down, shall he not much more
clothe you? If you have faith, God will know what you
have need of.' That's what the beggar said the Man of
Nazareth told a crowd of listeners. He was the happiest
beggar I ever saw."

"It's just as well you didn't tell Mother that, after her
talking about fine linen robes and all."

"But who wants fine linen and a pure white turban?"
Joanna interrupted her sister. "All I want is to be able
to walk like other people so strangers won't turn and
stare at me and so my own people won't pity me."

"I had an urge to follow him," Martha's shepherd boy
said after the three were quiet for a long time.

"Who, the beggar?" Martha asked.

"No, Jesus. The last story I heard made me have an
awful urge to try to find him."

"And leave me here without word? Why?" Joanna
turned to ask.

"And leave me, too?"

"Let me tell you. You'll know why when you hear."

"You can tell us tomorrow," Martha said. "We'll let our flock come near the shearing pens when you are there. I hear Mother turning on her bed; you must go now. You didn't mean you'd leave me here and follow him."

"And I wanted to tell Joanna about how the Man of Nazareth healed a Roman captain's friend—his servant, some said—without even going near him. That's why I had an urge to follow him."

"Mother is not stirring," Joanna half whispered. "Tell us, please."

"It's hard to believe, but I heard it three times: in the street, in the market, and at the gate in Nain.

"There was one of the Roman captains—centurions, the Romans call them. One of the hated Romans, now, mind you. One said his name was Caspius, and another said Petronius. But they could have gotten the names mixed up. And some said he was at the barracks in Tiberias; others said Bethsaida-Julias. There are Romans stationed at both locations. So from either place to Capernaum, where the incident took place, would be almost a half-day's journey.

"Anyway, the Roman captain found the Man of Nazareth in Capernaum. He told the healer that his friend or servant—some said one; some said the other—was desperately ill and dying of a fever. 'Where is he?' the Man of Nazareth asked. The Roman told him his friend was too ill to bring. Then the Roman called him 'Master.' Now the Romans don't call anybody Master. 'Master,' he said, 'it is quite a distance, and I didn't mean that you have to go to him. All you have to do is give an order, and he will be made well again. Or maybe because I am used to giving orders and seeing them carried out, I have offended you. I know that you can heal him, Master.'

" 'Surely you have not offended me,' is what Jesus answered the Roman.

"Then the Roman said, probably knowing that Jesus would be in trouble with his own people if he were seen with a hated Roman, 'I shouldn't have bothered you, Master, for I know I am not worthy of having you come into my house.' "

Joanna shifted her wooden sandal on the stone, but did not speak.

"And then Jesus said, 'In all the land I have found no faith as great as yours.' He said that to a Roman, with all the Man of Nazareth's own countrymen listening, hating the Roman. Jesus must have seen their hard looks. But he said, 'Go your way and worry no more. Because you have believed, what you have asked is done.' And they say the dying servant was healed at that very minute. It's hard to believe that a miracle like that could happen without the man's even having to see him or touch him.

"That's why I had an urge to follow and try to find him. I would have called him Master too. I would have said, 'I have heard about the wonderful thing you did for the Roman captain, the healing of his servant. I am only a shepherd from the central hill country. But there we have heard of you and have wished that you would come into our region. There I have a friend: gentle, guileless, and a burden to her mother, the sister of my betrothed. She is beautiful except that she was born maimed. She has a club foot and a withered arm, lifeless. She wanted to come to find you herself, but a long journey with a heavy wooden sandal on her twisted foot is hard. I know that you can heal her.' Those are the very words I would have said."

"If only it had happened," Joanna choked out. Benjamin placed his hand on her shoulder. "If it had happened, we would have been in the high pasture," Martha said, taking up the story. "We would have left the flock and, holding hands, raced down to Mother in the fields. I would have had a hard time keeping up with you. Mother would have dropped her hoe in the middle of the row and run to us."

"Or leaned on it and fainted," Benjamin added. Feeling Joanna's shoulder leave his hand as she bent forward, resting her head against her lamb to hide her tears, he went back to his story.

"The people were very disturbed that Jesus had shown favor to a Roman. And when they railed against him, especially the priest in Capernaum, Jesus said to them: 'I will do no more deeds in the midst of doubters and in the houses of unbelievers.' This he said right to the priest's face; then he left the town.

"Now the people of Capernaum were trying to build a new synagogue; and Caspius or Petronius, whoever the Roman man was, gave them money to finish it. That's what they said."

"Mother is stirring; she'll call for us. You must go now." Martha rose and pulled Benjamin after her. Joanna gently pushed her orphan lamb down the steps. "We'll see you at the shearing pen tomorrow," Martha said to Benjamin.

"Don't let the latch fall in the keeper." She now spoke quietly to Joanna, who had pushed the lamb out among the sleeping animals. "The lamb will start bleating if it rattles."

Chapter Three

Joanna pulled her rush mat from where it lay beside her sister. She noiselessly adjusted the inverted bowl that covered the fire pit so that a thin rim of glow made the dark penetrable. The half-light picked up the folds of Martha's coverlet, but lost itself at the edge of the mother's bed. Joanna lay with her withered side toward the opening between the fire pit and its cover. That side was always the first to chill. She had felt the night chill numb her foot and arm as she sat listening to Benjamin talk of the Man from Nazareth. His words had sent a freezing anxiety—yet a warming hope— through her whole body.

The only sound came from the dark beyond the edge of her mother's bed. Out of the blackness she heard the low breathing of her mother. It was deep and fitful— deep with weariness. Its fitfulness bespoke a troubled mind, a bosom that lifted and let slowly fall upon it again a heavy burden of pity and discontent.

She remembered her mother before this bitterness had possessed her, when Joanna was still a little girl and before her father was killed. "Do not come to the

high pasture," her mother would say. "Stay and play in the fields." And the gentle, wistful look on the child's face persuaded her mother to allow her to go.

Then, coming to some steep, stony part of the path, her mother would say, "Here, I must carry you over the rough spot." And always Joanna's withered side was cradled in against her mother's warm bosom. A feeling of strength and certainty was poured from one to the other. There surged through the child a dream that when her mother put her down she could run or skip and take wide steps, calling back, "See, Mother, see, I'm way ahead."

Was all her mother's change because her father had been killed? Was part of it knowing that Joanna was a girl now? She was no longer a child to be loved. Now she was to be pitied because there would never be any love for her except her mother's and her sister's. Joanna thought to herself, *One day I'll say to her, "Mother, I wish you would still treat me as a child. You hurt me when you talk of my being a girl now. When you talk that way I feel that I am a burden. I know you don't mean to appear ashamed of me; but I realize that having an unwed daughter is a sorrow to you. When Martha and Benjamin are married, I'll be a comfort to you. What do we care if people pity us because it is the custom that parents must marry off their daughters?"*

What if Benjamin had followed the Man from Nazareth? The matted rushes gave off the sound of a leaf turned by the wind as Joanna moved her sleepless body on the mat. *Suppose the great and wonderful healer had said, "You've come all the way from the hill country of Mount Sela to ask me to heal your friend?*

*You have great faith. It is done." And I, walking behind
the flock, would have suddenly been walking lopsided,
my wooden sandal making my leg too long. And without thinking I would have bent down and untied the
sandal strap with the wrong hand. Then I would have
stood straight up and seen that both hands were alike. I
would have stepped fearfully at first, then raced to find
Mother in the fields. She would think I was some
stranger until I called out.*

"Are you asleep, Martha?" Joanna asked in a
whisper. The heavy breathing of her mother had
slowed to a peaceful cadence; she was deep in slumber.
Joanna was wide awake; sleep was far away.

She sat up and gazed at the crack between the fire
cover and the brazier. She must cover the fire or it
would die. Then Martha would have to go and borrow
coals from Benjamin's house. While she considered
risking waking the others and covering the fire, the
last thin thread of glow turned to darkness.

Now she sat in that darkness, pondering all that
Benjamin had said. The wonder and brightness of her
waking dream was gone with the embers' glow. Her lip
began to quiver, and she clamped it between her teeth.
The inside of her throat swelled; she choked. She swallowed but dared not cough. The lump of agony would not
go down; it hurt her breathing. She let her lip go free,
and she formed words. She swallowed them, and they
pushed the lump before them somewhere down inside
her. *I'll go and find him myself. Now.*

At the door she lifted the latch quietly from its
keeper. The wooden hinges sounded their muffled
groan. She listened. There was no movement behind

her. She took her robe from where it hung beside the door, then picked up her wooden sandal and placed it on the step outside. She almost lost her balance, but the doorjamb steadied her. Her leather sandal she held in her hand, her robe over her arm; she slipped noiselessly through the door. Without a sound she put her robe and sandal down. Inch by inch she pulled the door toward her. The hinges groaned, but no louder than the hum of an angry bee.

She reached for the latchstring to lift the latch and let it slip ever so gently into its keeper. Then she must remember to push the latchstring back through its hole. Her mother was always annoyed if they left the latchstring out. Her fingers moved over the surface of the door, made smooth by use, where the latchstring hung. It wasn't there. She had forgotten to put it out.

Now she dared scarcely breathe; someone stirred inside. The door was still open enough to let a crack of moonlight show. If whoever was stirring woke up, she would see Joanna in the moonlight. If Joanna didn't latch the door, the chill night breeze would open it. Her mother would feel the chill and wake up before she was beyond the village gate. She'd make her come back. Her mother would use first harsh words, then sorrowful ones.

Inch by inch she widened the opening between the door and its post. When it was wide enough for half of her body, she pivoted on her good foot, felt in the dark with her good hand, and slowly inched the latchstring through its hole to the outside.

There was no stirring from within. The deep, wearied breathing of her mother faded behind the **door** as she eased it noiselessly into its place and, without a sound, let the latch slip into its keeper. She worked the latchstring back through its hole. Martha and her mother were safe against intruders.

Joanna wrapped her robe about her. On the lower step she sat down and tied on her sandals. The moon picked out the motionless animals in the courtyard. The girl tossed her head slightly, and her long hair fell into place about her shoulders. Her browned cheeks and dark eyes, lighted by the soft, silver light, gave off a determined half-smile. It died in an instant.

Her orphan lamb had sensed her presence. Now she heard a low bleat, followed by a louder one, and a small white form came toward her from among the sleeping animals. "Rachel," the girl whispered, and she quickly cradled the lamb in her arms. Rubbing its head with her lifeless hand, she made her way to the gate. "Rachel, Rachel," she whispered, "you must be quiet now." But Rachel understood only her movement. As Joanna stooped to put her down, Rachel set up a stream of bleating. She was used to being carried through the gate and partway to the hill pasture. She was never left behind.

Joanna studied the door, expecting it to open. She stood for a long time. Now she tried again. "You must be quiet and stay this one time," she whispered. But Rachel was spoiled in her creature ways and set up another fitful chorus of bleating. "Then I'll let you go with me," the girl whispered. "And if someone takes you for the Passover sacrifice, it won't be my fault."

Once safely through the gate and past several houses along the path that led to the south gate of the village, she put the lamb down. It now followed without a bleat.

Joanna was not afraid. Outside the village gate she took the ridge road south toward Jerusalem. Far in the distance she saw the specks of campfires, which were common sights at Passover time. The road was never lonely during Passover, and the hills were always dotted with the fires of people camping along the way. Their donkeys brayed, and their sacrificial lambs bleated. Everyone made the journey if they could. Joanna had been several times before her father died; then they had had a donkey for her to ride. She could find her way to Rebecca Mark's house. She would see Rhoda and John Mark. They would help her find the Man from Nazareth.

"I could say to him"—now she was in the open country and spoke aloud to Rachel—"if you will heal me, I'll give you my pet lamb for your Passover."

Rachel bounced about in the moonlight. She nosed a thornbush at the edge of the road and backed away. "After all, you might have gotten me caught," Joanna said. "And you're only a pet lamb. You'll grow up and go with the flock. Every year there's an orphan or two. I'll have another one next year when you are grown and only remember sometimes how you came to beg to have your head rubbed. Don't get in front of me or I'll trip over you."

Joanna gathered her robe more closely about her. The sway of her body as she limped caused the robe to slip down from her withered shoulder. The clop-clop-clop of her thick-soled sandal made a sort of rhythm. She was going at a good pace. Her thoughts were of the

Healer. "But Benjamin didn't say he asked anything for his healing," she said aloud to the orphan lamb. "When we come back, you'll have to run to keep up."

Now she was nearly opposite the first campfire she had seen from the village gate. She stopped and looked back at the cluster of houses, faded now to dim checkers of light against the hills as the moon shone on their flat marl roofs. "When we get tired we'll ask to warm at somebody's fire," she said to the lamb, then set her face toward Jerusalem. The clop of her wooden sandal measured a quickened, lively step.

Chapter Four

Joanna walked on and on. Following the flock to the pasture, she would often stop and rest because a dull pain would start where the bones of her ankle turned her foot inward. The pain would rise to an aching throb and climb through that side of her body. So far, no pain.

Even though she felt the night chill, she did not turn aside to any of the campfires she passed. In the dim light of some she noted a circle of forms sleeping on the ground. Nearby would be a donkey standing with head down, asleep or reaching for grass at the end of its tight tether.

But at some camps there were no donkeys. She would fall in with one of these groups, a group with small children who wouldn't be moving too fast for her. She wouldn't pick out a family with a donkey; they might think they should let her ride, and they'd be embarrassed.

Several times she stopped and listened in the direction she had come. If her mother awoke and found her gone, would she hurry through the night to make her go back? She imagined she heard her mother calling far behind—"Jo-anna, Jo-an-na." Rachel came close and rubbed against her when she stopped to listen. "It's my imagination," she reassured herself aloud.

What if her mother sent Benjamin or Martha in the morning? She would be so far along that they would turn back. She was going almost as fast as anybody else could walk. She would have such a start by morning, if the pain didn't start, that they wouldn't be able to catch up.

What would she say to the faith healer? First she would have to find him in all the crowds of people. He would be near the Temple. Everybody crowded into the Temple grounds. Rhoda and John Mark would help her find him. They would have heard about him. Rhoda would help her. Maybe John Mark wouldn't. He was two years older than she was. Once she had asked him to let her go with him into the Street of the Bazaars, where there was always excitement and lots of sweet smells and pretty trinkets to look at. But he had looked at her wooden sandal and then run off with his friends. However, that had been three years ago, when she was still a child. And John Mark was only two years older. He'd be sixteen now. He would help her find the Man from Nazareth. But what if Rhoda didn't work at her mother's cousin's house anymore and was gone? If John Mark was still not nice? *Martha calls Benjamin her shepherd boy,* Joanna thought, *and Benjamin is nice. Maybe John Mark will be like him now that he's older.*

There'll be others looking for him, anyway. I'll just ask in the street, "Do you know where the faith healer called Jesus is?" In big towns like Jerusalem there's always a gate that people call the Gate of Sorrows. The lepers who can't come into the city live and beg there. And the crippled and the blind, too. The poor, too, I guess. That's why Mother is always saying, "The Gate of Sorrows leads nowhere." The Man from Nazareth might be there if he's like Benjamin says—healing all the people. And I'll just push my way up to him and say, "Master." Then I'll tell him, "I've walked all the way from Mount Sela because my sister's betrothed heard of you in Nain, and I know you can heal me." Then . . .

Joanna's thoughts filled up the night. A pink line of dawn threaded its way among the far hills on the other side of the Jordan. Here and there a chat finch began a soft chatter in the squat yews and thornbushes along the road. Rachel was beginning to get hungry; she would stop and nibble along the roadside, then race, bleating for Joanna to wait until she caught up.

The dawn added brightness and some cheer to Joanna's walking and to her hope. She talked aloud to the lamb. "If you don't keep up I know what I'll do. If the healer doesn't want you, I'll sell you outside the courtyard of the Temple. And if he's touched me and I'm healed, I might like to buy a new robe like Mother said. A snow-white shawl to hang about my shoulders would be nice.

"You're a fat, spoiled lamb. You would bring a good price. And that's what lambs are made for—to sell, not to be pets. But don't fret and bleat so much. I'll let you get your fill of grass. Maybe you're thirsty, too. I am. We'll find a water hole or a well when the sun is up. We couldn't see one in the night.

"When I can walk straight we'll go to the Street of

the Bazaars. You'll keep up with me then, for you'll want to follow the sweet smells. Some goldsmith will look at you and call to me, 'A pet for my child. How much do you want?' Then I'll trade you for a necklace and earrings—gold or silver or rich bright copper ones. I don't want pale, tiny brass. I'll make the goldsmith say he'll take good care of you.

"I'll need a necklace and earrings when I can dance. My necklace will sway and swing to the rhythm of my own shepherd boy's flute. I'll have someone like Martha's Benjamin then. My earrings will ring a soft tune in my ears when I dance at the Feast of the Tabernacles. We'll gather the grapes and tread out the wine at the winepress, where the blind man strums his lyre. All I've ever done before is sit flat on the ground, so people won't see my foot, and watch Martha dance with all the other girls. And Benjamin stands nearby, clapping his hands and waiting to wipe Martha's brow so softly with his napkin when the dance is over. Someone will be waiting for me. Then Benjamin won't have to help me over the stiles when we go home from the feast.

"I'll let Martha borrow my necklace or my earrings, whichever she wants. Benjamin will look at her with his eyes bright and soft. When he looks at me, I see the pity that darkens them.

"But come, you've got enough grass for now—I'm getting hungry, too. When the sun is up we'll stop at somebody's camp, and they'll ask us to share their barley cake. Then I'll rest in the sun. And you can graze your fill."

Joanna was beginning to tire. Her wooden sandal

was heavy now; the crooked bones were beginning to ache. The pink line of dawn widened, became an arch of greenish light, and then turned to gold. Day was bursting upon the hills. A song thrush, like the one Joanna listened to on the way to the hill pasture each morning, began to sing—mellow, flutelike, and far away. Joanna stood and listened, watching the day being born. The song thrush's notes made her feel warm, even though the sun was only a thin rim above the distant hills.

A little way along, a woman kneeling over a fire set between two stones called to her. A large barley cake warmed on a thin, flat stone that rested on the edges of the two stones that enclosed the fire. At the sound of the woman's voice there was a movement of blanket-covered bodies on the ground. *The father and three children,* Joanna thought. *And the children are big enough to keep up with their parents.*

Joanna shared their barley cake and answered the woman's many questions as to why she was walking alone. They, too, were hill people and had heard nothing of the Man from Nazareth. The father thought he was probably just another of the many fake healers who tried to live by their tricky wits rather than by honest work. By the time they had finished eating, Joanna had no desire to walk with them. She thanked the woman, then explained that she must wait for Rachel to graze longer. When they were gone she sat on the firestones and warmed herself.

Now and then she cast a look back over the way she had come. This was about the time Martha would be taking the flock to pasture. Her mother would be going to the fields. Benjamin would be testing the fleece in the shearing pen to see if the night's dew was dried off so he could begin the shearing. She wondered what they would think had happened to the orphan lamb.

But Martha and her mother would be going to their daily duties much later this morning. On awakening to find Joanna gone, her mother would send Martha through the village to bring Benjamin to overtake the "stubborn, dreaming child."

The woman herself had gone to the village and gazed a long time at the road that led south toward Jerusalem. Martha and Benjamin returned first, and Martha was the first to notice that Joanna's orphan lamb was not underfoot, trying to get in at the door. "Her lamb is gone," Martha had said when her mother came slowly across the animal yard. "I think she just might be vexed and feeling sad after the talk last night. She may have gone up into the hills. When I feel that way, sometimes I move apart from the flock and sit alone on a high rock. She wouldn't take that lamb to be a hindrance underfoot if she set out for Jerusalem."

"But I think we will let her go." The woman spoke with less harshness in her voice than when she had ordered Martha to bring Benjamin. "She has a mind of her own, but I keep thinking of her as a child. If we bring her back, she'll always be saying, 'If only—if only'; and we'll know little peace until she gets over it.

"At the village I saw some families moving on the road; perhaps no harm will come to her. My cousin Rebecca will welcome her. She'll stay her visit out and come home sheepish but perhaps contented. Then we'll hear no more of it; we'll keep our burdens in our hearts."

On the road Joanna walked slower than she had through the night. Several families passed her—some walking, some with small children on donkeys, some bearing men and women too old to walk. Some spoke. Once an old woman stopped her son, who was leading the donkey on which she rode. They had a whispered conversation. Joanna saw the man shake his head. Then as they started on, the old woman looked back and smiled a toothless smile. Joanna thought the old woman had asked her son if the donkey could carry double. She wondered if the old woman had been to the Passover all the years of her life.

A hard-faced man followed by a woman who looked always at the ground and whose body was bent with their provisions' pack, plus a dove cage with two doves tied at her side, passed but did not speak. And before they were out of hearing, Joanna heard the man say, "Why do the beggars and the maimed always clutter up the city every year at Passover time? They can't get into the Temple court anyway, can they? And her with a lamb for a sacrifice, to beg money at the court gate to have it blessed, I guess."

"We could have brought a lamb," the woman said, never raising her head. "We could have bought the doves there, too. You'll have to pay to have them blessed anyway."

Joanna did not hear the man's last words, but as he spoke them he turned and, with the side of his sandal, sent a cloud of dust back toward the woman. She trudged on after him, her head still lowered.

In the hills above the road Joanna noted the grazing flocks, some new shorn and white against the dappled green and brown of the hill pastures. Shepherds, framed against the sky or perched on a high rock, kept watch. Some closest to the road waved as she passed.

Twice she passed close enough to the circled walls of shearing pens to hear the nervous bleating from within them. Rachel heard them, too, and answered back a clipped bleat or two. The sun was hot, so when she rested she found a hawthorn bush tall enough for shade or turned aside to sit in the shadow of a great rock.

Toward evening a caravan passed on a wide road that led westward toward the falling sun. Perhaps because she was hungry and looked longingly at a sun-darkened, leather-faced driver who was eating pomegranates as he followed his camels, he stopped. Anyway, he reached into his sack, said, "Hold out your hands," and poured six pomegranates and two onions into them.

She sat for a long time eating, watching until the caravan disappeared in the low hills toward the valley. She thought the road must lead to Joppa. That was where the caravans sold their goods that went across the sea in ships, she knew. She wondered about the big world beyond the hills. The caravan driver was such a kind man. And he didn't look like her people. She wondered if he gave everybody pomegranates and onions. Rachel ate the pomegranate seeds from her palm and licked and licked to get the last drop of the sweet juice.

All day when Joanna had stopped to rest, she had cast anxious looks back the way she had come. Now she felt sure her mother had decided to let her go on. The sun was going down; Martha would be bringing the flock from the pasture; her mother would be coming from the fields.

The sun sank below the low hills in the west, and ripple-edged clouds turned red, then deepened into purple. The long shadows of the hills soaked into the ground and became part of night's earth.

I am now in the loneliest part of the road, she thought. No one had passed since the caravan driver. Along the entire road in both directions no campfires could be seen.

Her foot ached steadily now. But she would rest a little longer, then walk past the next ridge and hope to find a friendly fire for the night. Rachel picked at the grass among the stones and became a blurred speck of white against them.

Joanna moved to the sheltered side of a tall rock. The chill breeze that comes with night was rising. She gathered her robe close about her and stretched it down to cover her feet.

At home the milking would be finished now. Martha would be washing the milk jars. Her mother would be kneading dough for supper. For a moment she was lonely and homesick and afraid. She wondered if they were talking about how far she was on her way. She wondered if her mother would scold her and say, "I told you so" if she didn't find the Man from Nazareth and go home rejoicing. She *would* find him.

Her eyelids grew heavy and began to droop. Rachel

became a gray blur among the rocks. Joanna called to her; but her lips and her chin were heavy, too. Only a mumbled whisper escaped her lips. Curled in against the great stone, still warm from the day's burning sun, she was asleep.

Fatigue and warmth make sleep that takes command of pain and fear and hides agonies of day under the night's dreams. So now she dreamed.

Above the shelter rock and looking down, three people stood. In her dream the forms slowly took shape. Judith, her mother, her eyes glistening with tears, spoke; and Joanna remembered the voice she had heard when her mother carried her, as a child, against her warm bosom home from the fields at evening. "We're going with you—all the way." And Martha and Benjamin, bending down and reaching out, spoke as one. "Here, we brought you food."

"Barley loaf, fresh from the oven, baked with honey and leavened; and fig cake," Martha said as she held out the bread. The glazed coating of honey, rich and brown, shone as though it had been polished.

"And here a skin of milk to drink with it, still warm from milking," Benjamin said as he passed into her good hand a small skin of milk.

When fatigue ebbs out of sleep, pain returns. The night cold that puts an end to warmth brings to the sleeper a numbed anxiety and restless stirring. The sleeping sheep moves from its place atop the flat stone where it has bedded down. It moves down to the earth at the windless side of the rock; paws the earth twice to see that it is smooth; turns once full circle, looking at the ground; then settles down to sleep again. Bleatless,

it moves. The shepherd knows the harmless stirring, unlike the frightened uprising and nervous bleating when the wolf or jackal is near.

The moon was up and high above the hills. Joanna had slept a long time. The earth was sleeping, too. The face of the shelter rock against which the girl lay had grown cold. She stirred. Cold said wake up; fatigue said sleep. She slept a troubled sleep between the two and dreamed.

A terrible argument was going on between Joanna and Martha. Their mother, Judith, had died of a delirious fever. The plague that seldom reached into the hill country had come. It had started in Bucolon on the sea and had spread death in a wide swath along the plain and into the hills. They had dug her grave in the burial ground outside the village wall. Benjamin had helped because the ground was very rocky. He also had gone among the neighbors to beg resin of wormwood to seal the graveclothes because there were no ointments and spices.

Joanna sobbed in her sleep. She stirred and gathered her robe more closely about her. In her dream Martha was crying aloud because their mother's graveclothes were of coarse goat's hair and not fine linen.

Now she and Martha were filling the grave. Benjamin and all their friends had been sent away because only the family could perform the last sacred duty of folding a loved one back into the earth.

So many stones had been removed that there was not enough earth to fill the grave. Now an argument arose between the two. Joanna wanted to use the stones to finish the filling. "They will keep scavengers, hyenas

and jackals, from disturbing the body." But Martha, weeping aloud, kept repeating, "We'll carry earth in baskets from the fields."

Joanna awoke with a start—she heard a muffled scream or cry, like that of a child fighting the dark when the blanket covers its head. "Rachel! Rachel!" Joanna screamed as she scrambled to her feet.

The sound had come from above the road, where she had last seen the lamb picking grass among the stones. *That terrible dream,* she thought. "Rachel, Rachel," she called again and searched the stones in the moonlight. Now she heard a low growl and a rustle among the bushes.

She stumbled among the rocks; her sandals were on the ground by the stone where she had fallen asleep. She clambered up the steep slope on her hands and feet. "Rachel, Rachel." No more choked cries came to her.

Between two stones where she had found shelter, Rachel lay struggling. She kicked in her death throes; in her last convulsions for breath she arched and straightened her tiny body, her white fleece now blotched with blood in the moonlight. Then one last straightening of her body and a fitful pawing of the air with one front leg, and the lamb moved no more. Far away a jackal barked; another answered it.

Joanna sat on a rock above the still lamb. She did not begin to weep. She did not look down; she did not notice that the moon was low in the western sky. She was not aware that she had slept so long, that the night was dying.

The location barks of the jackals brought them to-

gether. Now the sharp bark turned to a wailing howl far back in the scrub. Joanna listened, gathered several small throwing-stones within her reach, and waited. Other fears possessed her. The terrifying dream of her mother being dead and the loss of the lamb were ill omens. The hope with which she had begun her journey and the courage to go on were gone. She would turn back.

Chapter Five

Dawn came bloodred. When the sun was up, the kites and ravens came. The screaming of the kites, racing in ever-nearing circles above Joanna and the lamb, filled the morning air and drowned out the singing of the chat finches and thrushes. The brazen ravens chattered and fussed among themselves, preening their feathers and stretching their wings almost within a stone's throw of Joanna. "How do they always know?" the girl said aloud. "Let a lamb be born in the pasture and the birth blood draws them before the mother has nuzzled the lamb to its wobbly legs to find milk."

On the way back to the shelter rock to get her sandals, Joanna searched the ground for a thin stone with a sharp point that she could use to dig. When she found one, she scooped out a grave between the stones where the lamb lay. As she placed its stiff body at the bottom of the grave, she began to sob. She tamped the earth tight over it with her wooden sandal.

Her dream came back to her. Up the slope she found a large, flat stone that she could move but not lift. She slid it over the grave, bruising her fingers as its edge caught them against other stones. The kites and ravens would have no feast. She wondered if the jackals would come again with nightfall.

People used wormwood resin on burial clothes when they didn't have spices and ointments; it, like the spices, repelled the scavengers. Why had she wanted to cover her mother's grave with stones? She sat by the road and pondered the awful dream again. "It has no meaning," she said aloud. The sun was warm now. "The dream came from sleeping against the cold stone." The sun made her feel better.

She would go on. She would find the Man from Nazareth. She stood a long time, studying the road in both directions. Far to the north there were people on the road. Three forms—could her first dream be coming true? She was hungry. Could they be her mother and Martha and Benjamin? She waited.

Soon she could make them out, a man and woman with a donkey, carrying three small children. When they were almost to her the man shaded his eyes and studied the sky. "Something dead," he said to the woman.

"There's a girl," one of the children said, pointing.

When they came abreast, the woman smiled and spoke. "You are alone, child?"

"Yes," Joanna answered and stepped forward. The children stared at the strange sandal.

"You can stretch a little," the man said as he began to lift the children to the ground.

"We're going to the Passover." The woman spoke now to Joanna, then called to the smallest child, who was trying to follow the others up the rough slope. "Come back, Sarah."

"I'm going to the Passover, too," Joanna said and continued. "Not so much for the Passover, but to find Jesus, the healer, in Jerusalem. My sister's betrothed brought word from Nain that he had left the north country and gone to Jerusalem. I have faith that he can heal me so I can walk straight."

The man stood studying the circling kites.

"Something dead," the woman said.

"I had a lamb. Jackals killed it last night when I fell asleep."

"Poor child," the man interrupted. He added, "You're hungry." Without waiting for an answer, he took a barley loaf from his pack and passed it to Joanna. "Take all you want," he said. "We're from Cana. We started late, but we'll get there in time to celebrate the feast."

"We're from Cana," the woman repeated. "We know about the mighty works of the healer, Jesus. He will heal you."

Joanna broke off a small piece of bread and returned the loaf to the man. "You are kind," she said. "Last night I dreamed I was eating honey bread, and now I am."

"It's better to keep the children quiet on the road," the woman said. "They get tired riding, and they get tired walking. When we fix camp they're never hungry, but once we break camp they ask for food. Little Sarah is forgiven; she's only three. Joseph and David are five and six and should know better. Josiah says to me, 'Hannah, it's no harm to pamper them a little.' But

I know when we're back home Josiah will be in the fields, and I'll be the one who's pestered.

"We'll let the boys follow until they tire, and you will ride with Sarah." The woman nodded to Josiah as she spoke. A gentle smile from the man gave Joanna assurance.

"Come, Joseph and David, we're ready to move on," the man called to the boys still among the rocks.

"I don't want to take their place," was all Joanna could think to say. And before she had finished she was helped astride Barak, the donkey, whom Josiah called by name and ordered to stand still. Sarah, the child, was lifted up behind her. The man adjusted the pack that swung on either side behind the child.

Joanna was now a part of a pilgrimage. She would watch very carefully; and when Joseph and David began to whine and lag, she would insist that kind Hannah and Josiah go on. But for now she need have no worry. As they moved along Hannah called to the boys, "Don't run too far ahead."

Joanna whispered the woman's words over to herself. They were nothing special to the woman or the boys who heard them and slackened their pace. *But one day, one day,* Joanna thought, *in the fields or to or from the pastures, Mother will have to call to me: "Don't run too far ahead."*

Joanna could not decide whether Josiah let Barak set the pace or if the man did it by a gentle tug on the halter rope (which she could not detect). Once or twice the boys fell behind, and the father called to them. When they caught up, they gave their mother flowers: wild flax, blue as the sky, rock iris, and field lilies.

The man and woman talked to each other of the Man from Nazareth. They spoke of how in their own town, Cana, he had been at a wedding feast where the wine had run out. He had turned water into wine, they said. And in Capernaum he had healed a man possessed of a demon. Joanna listened intensely.

Josiah and Hannah had not been at the wedding feast. They had never seen him; but they knew several young men, fishermen from Galilee, who believed in him so much that they had given up their jobs to follow him about the country.

Joanna felt the grip of Sarah's little hands slacken on her robe. She reached back with her good arm and held the dozing child.

The pace of Barak was slowing; several groups of pilgrims passed. The boys were trudging farther behind and calling more often for them to wait. Joanna studied the sun; it was halfway up the sky.

When Josiah stooped and let Joseph climb on his back, Joanna spoke to the man. "David is tired, too. You've helped me enough. I have plenty of time. You must be there to celebrate the feast. And I want only to find Jesus, the healer. I'll go to my mother's cousin's house and wait until the crowds have thinned after the celebrations. I can find him easier then."

"No. When the sun is high we'll stop to rest and let Barak graze. David is not dragging yet."

Joanna thought she might tell them that it didn't hurt her to walk, but she kept quiet. She would tell them that when her foot was kept in one position too long, it began to hurt. This would be the truth. She hadn't ridden since she was a child. Her foot, dangling at Barak's flank, was beginning to ache.

"You must ride like a princess," the woman said as she came close beside Joanna, her voice all tenderness. Smiling, she held out to Joanna the flowers the boys had brought to her. Joanna, holding Sarah with her good arm, now for the first time took her withered hand from under her robe. The woman did not let her smile fade in pity, as Joanna had seen so many times in others' eyes. "We have much more to tell you of the Man from Nazareth yet. Josiah heard firsthand, from people who had actually seen the wonder he did at Bethmaus, near Galilee. You tell it, Josiah. I might not get it just the right way."

Josiah had been walking slightly behind and had not seen Joanna take the flowers with her withered hand. "You meant when he healed the man with the withered hand on the sabbath?"

"I meant the time he cured Jairus' little girl," the woman interrupted.

"That was afterward, but in about the same locality."

"But tell that one," the woman said. "It is so lovely, and the girl wasn't much younger than Joanna here."

"Jesus had been teaching and preaching on the other side of the Sea of Galilee. When he came back across, a group of people were waiting on the shore for him. Jairus, a ruler of the synagogue in Bethmaus, was among them. He'd spent most of the day waiting, walking on the shore, watching.

"When Jesus stepped out of the boat, Jairus ran to him and fell down on his knees. He said, 'Master, my little daughter is at the point of death. She is dying, and she is my only daughter. I pray you, come with me and lay your hands on her that she may be made well and live.'

"Jesus went with him. And all the crowd followed, too. As they neared the house where the sick child was, Jesus stopped and asked the crowd to go back. Even while he was doing this, someone came running from Jairus' house and said to Jairus, 'You need not trouble him to come any farther; the child is dead.'

"Jesus turned to Jairus and said, 'Fear not; only believe' and went walking right on toward the house. When they got there some neighbors had already gathered outside and were weeping and wailing. Jesus looked at them and said, 'Why are you creating all this tumult and weeping? The child is not dead. She is only asleep.'

"Then the people began to laugh and make scornful remarks to him. He asked Jairus not to let any of them follow him into the house. So he went in with Jairus and the three followers of Jesus, the young men we told you about who left their jobs on the fishing boats to go with him. When Jesus had come to the bedside where the child's mother stood weeping over her, he reached down and took the child's hand and said, 'Little girl, I say unto you, arise.'

"And the twelve-year-old girl got up and walked. Then he told her parents to give her something to eat. He told Jairus not to tell anybody what he had done. But as soon as the people outside saw Jairus, they could tell what had happened. And the healer's fame was greater from that moment.

"I heard the story from one of the neighbors. He said

Jairus was following Jesus out of the house, trying to get him to take some gift wrapped in doeskin; but Jesus refused."

Joanna saw through her quiet tears that the sun was at its height. David was having to be urged along by his mother's quiet words. It was time for her to insist that they had helped her enough. But she wanted to hear more. "Why did he not want anybody told about his great work?" she said.

"Well, some time before he healed Jairus' little girl, he had gotten in trouble with the Pharisees for breaking the sabbath. That was the story I started to tell you before."

The same story Benjamin heard, Joanna thought. *It has to be true.* Her eyes shone like diamonds.

The woman studied the bright hope that shone in Joanna's eyes as she listened. This time she did not interrupt Josiah.

"On the sabbath Jesus had gone into the synagogue to teach. Now there was a man there who had a withered hand, his right hand. Jesus knew that the Pharisees were in league with Herod and wanted to get something against him.

"When Jesus came to the man with the withered hand, he asked him to stand up. Then Jesus, knowing what the Pharisees were thinking, turned and spoke to them. 'Is it lawful on the sabbath day to do good, or to do harm? To save a life, or to kill? If a man had a sheep that got caught in the brambles or fell into a ditch on its back, wouldn't that man save it even though it was the sabbath? Isn't a man worth more than a sheep? Then isn't it right to heal on the sabbath day?' But the

Pharisees only watched; they didn't answer him.

"So he said to the man with the withered hand, 'Stretch out your hand.' When the man reached out his hand it had been healed, made whole just like his other one. Jesus didn't even touch it. The man went away rejoicing, but the Pharisees went away plotting how they could report Jesus to Herod and have him arrested and put to death, as Herod had done to John the Baptist."

"I know it is true," Joanna said; then she caught herself and said no more. Josiah went on with his story.

"I guess that's why he asked Jairus not to let it be known that his child had been healed. You see, a lot of the Pharisees' followers were going over to Jesus."

The woman had watched Joanna's face. There was no sign of embarrassment at hearing talk about a withered hand.

"We'll rest awhile," the man said, as he noticed that David's feet were sending up little puffs of dust as he dragged one after the other.

"And I must walk," Joanna said. "When I have been too long in one position, my crippled foot begins to hurt."

Josiah and Hannah protested, but Joanna would not relent. "You must get to the Temple court to buy your sacrifice before it closes tomorrow at sundown. You have helped me and given me new heart. I was ready to turn back before you came."

Finally, seeing that Joanna could not be persuaded, the man took from his pack the barley loaf from which Joanna had earlier eaten a small portion. "Then this is all we can do for you?" he asked, pressing it into the girl's hands.

Joanna sat by the roadside and watched as the three forms became a blur in the heat waves that rose from the earth. When they were lost among the great rocks that edged the road, she began to walk. She caught herself looking back to see where Rachel was. She smiled through her tears and quickened her pace.

Chapter Six

She walked the whole afternoon, until the sun was far down, and only rested twice. She wondered how far Josiah and Hannah had gotten. She thought the Man from Nazareth would be like them when she found him.

No one passed along the way now. She knew from hearing her parents talk, before her father was dead and during the time when they went to Jerusalem for the Passover, that people liked to get there a day early. They sang psalms around the campfires and enjoyed the carnival atmosphere before the solemn ceremonies of the feast. Also, they bought sacrifices in the Temple court before the lambs and doves were picked over and the best were gone.

"Now my path is strewn with flowers," she said aloud and smiled. She saw in the road the flowers Hannah had given her when she said, "You must ride like a princess." Joanna had given them to Sarah after her father had lifted her up and set her on Barak when they were leaving. The child had grown drowsy; her grasp must have loosened. The rock iris and the field

as Joanna kept on with her clop-clop-clop in the dark, began to slow her steps. But her thoughts were winged, soaring the night sky, finding their way among the stars, riding the breeze.

What would she say to the Man from Nazareth? Would he call her "Little girl," as he had said to Jairus' daughter? Suppose he had come to fear the officials so much that he had stopped healing people? He didn't want the news to get out that he had healed the little girl. If he said, "No, I can do no more great things because I don't want to end up like John the Baptist," she would burst out weeping before his very eyes. No, she would not let him see her cry.

If she went home healed and her mother prepared a feast to celebrate, all the neighbors would whisper among themselves, "See, Joanna is dancing." Her mother would be filled with joy. And when they walked together, her mother would sing the way she used to sing:

> I will lift up my eyes to the hills.
> From whence does my help come?
> My help comes from the Lord,
> > Who made heaven and earth.
>
> He will not let your foot be moved,
> > he who keeps you will not slumber.
> . . . .
> The Lord is your keeper;
> > the Lord is your shade
> > on your right hand.
> The sun shall not smite you by day,
> > nor the moon by night.

The Lord will keep you from all evil;
    he will keep your life.
The Lord will keep
      your going out and your coming in
      from this time forth and for evermore.
        (Ps. 121)

And when her mother had finished singing she would say, " 'He will not suffer your foot to be moved' means he will not let me stumble or fall when I am carrying you, my child." But that was long ago.

Josiah and Hannah would be singing the same hymn up the last hill as they came in sight of the city. "All the pilgrims sing it when they come in sight of the city on the way to the Passover," her mother had told her. Judith had learned it when she was a girl, when she went from Bethel each year with her father and mother.

Had her mother stopped singing because she thought the mention of "your foot" would hurt Joanna's feelings? Joanna stumbled all the time. Or had the songs ceased when her father had been killed? Joanna could not remember.

"When I come near the city, I will sing, too." Joanna was speaking aloud to the night. "And if there are other people going up, they will stare at me. But I won't care. I'll sing anyway."

Last night she had fallen asleep before the moon came up. Now she was still walking, and the moon was high above the hills. Its light dimmed the stars. Except for the brightest ones, it took the whole sky for itself. There were no campfires on the horizon. All the pilgrims still on the road would be past Bethel so they could make it to Jerusalem early the next day.

Joanna wondered how far it was yet to Bethel. Had she missed it in the dark? It lay off to the west of the road. No, she wouldn't have missed it. It was close enough to the road for the night breeze to carry the smells and sounds to her. She knew village smells and the yelps of wild scavenger dogs that disturbed the night outside village walls.

The dull pain that came from walking far now began to throb in her side. She would rest and start again at dawn. She found a shelter rock away from the night wind. She drew her knees up and tucked her robe about her feet. She held the portion of her barley loaf inside the folds of her robe so that night creatures would not smell it and come prowling around.

The winsome, almost pleading call of a tawny owl, so different from the doleful mourning of the night-hag she had heard earlier, lightened the heavy night silence. She tested her eyelids; sleep seemed far away. The peace and excitement of this day had not loaded them with heaviness.

She studied the shapes and shadows around her. A thin young juniper, clipped by hungry roebucks and gazelles, looked like a man standing. *It stands erect as my father did against the skyline in the high pasture,* she thought. He would carry her home in the twilight, teaching her the signs and wonders of the earth— where the ravens roost at night, the smell of henna and myrtle sending their sweet perfume up from the earth when the dew moistens their leaves. And at evening, when the work was finished, he would carry her up to the rooftop of the house. She never feared that he would stumble. Sometimes he would point to the stars and call them by name. If bleating arose in the animal yard below, disturbing the evening's quiet, he would call his sheep by name. They would listen and return to chewing their cuds. He would speak of peaceful toil. He never seemed to be weary.

Her mother didn't go up to the rooftop, not since he had died. Was his absence the reason, or was it because Joanna found the steep steps so hard to mount without her father to carry her? *Mother's eyes are always heavy, and she always nods as she sits at evening by the fire pit, like mine did last night,* Joanna thought. *Worry and troublesome toil make the eyes heavy.*

"I am too excited to sleep," Joanna whispered half-aloud. "If my foot didn't hurt I could walk the whole night."

Something moved—a shadow formed among the rocks below her. She listened. A wheezy, snortlike sniffing came to her. *A hated jackal, a hyena!* No, those creatures smelled only blood and carrion. *A bear! I'll throw the bread far down the hill and run. It smells the honey bread.* But the shadow was too small for a bear. She felt the earth around her for a small stone and threw it in the direction from which the sniffing had come. There was a rustle in the tares that grew among the stones, then quiet. She listened. *A harmless badger!* "Of all animals, the most shy," her father had once said.

The tawny owl's pleading night call had stopped. The moon climbed higher and higher above the holy hills of Israel, shortening their night shadows, keeping watch over silent sheepfolds crowning their crests and far-scattered villages, spilling over the slopes, their flat marl roofs reflecting back to the moon its brightness. And the moon, too, kept watch over the still form under Joanna's robe. Fatigue and exciting hope had ceased their differences and come together. Joanna was asleep and dreamless.

Chapter Seven

Joanna awoke with a start. A terrible dream! People all around her! Tumult on the road! Loud laughter! The clank of metal! The measured thud of tramping feet!

No, it was not a dream. Almost upon her on the road above was a column of soldiers. The polished plates on their leather corselets shone in the sun. She had slept through the night; the sun was already above the hills.

She would lie still, and maybe they wouldn't see her. No, they would pass too close. She was only a few cubits below the road and was facing it. She would crawl quickly and hide among the stones. She moved on her hands and knees.

Something held her fast. She jerked. She had gone to sleep without untying her sandal straps. Her wooden sandal was wedged in the crevice of a great flat stone upon which she lay sprawled, in full view of the road. She pulled; she tried to lift her foot. The pain was more than she could bear. She pushed her body back to ease the tension, pulled her robe over her head, and scarcely breathed.

The tramp of feet slowed to a shuffle. The rattle of

metal stopped. The voices and laughter died and became a mumble—low but unbroken, like a wind's incessant whisper.

Her whole body trembled, and her teeth chattered. *Savage and murderous Romans—if I had only listened to Mother* ran through her mind. *I'll tell them I've just come from Bethel, not far away, looking for sheep that escaped from the fold. I'll hurry down the hill, calling as I go. Then I'll hide, and they'll be gone.*

A hand touched the robe and slowly folded it back from her head. "You gave us quite a fright." With eyes still wide with fear and streaming tears, she looked up into the face of the man smiling down at her. "Don't you know it's dangerous to camp without a fire in this lonely country? You could have been torn to pieces by wild beasts. And you alone here."

The hand that had folded back her robe now rested gently on her shoulder. "You don't have to be afraid. It is day. No harm will come to you now." And as he spoke he put his crested helmet, which he had held in the crook of his arm, upon the ground. He reached out and took her hand, still gripping the edge of the stone.

The mumbling behind her became quiet voices. She heard the shuffle of feet. "Do you need any help, sir?" came from the road.

The stranger lifted her arm as though to help her rise, speaking over his shoulder as he did. "No, it's only a scared little girl, lost."

Joanna's teeth had stopped their chattering. Her lips no longer quivered. The soft warmth of the stranger's hand upon her shoulder had stilled her trembling. At last she could speak. "I can't get up; my sandal is caught in the crack of the rock."

"I'll help you." The stranger now bent over her. The heavy nails of his thick-soled sandals scraped upon the stone. He twisted her wooden sandal. "Tell me if it hurts," he said.

He worked so gently that she felt no pain. Her foot was free. She sat up. The stranger moved his helmet aside and knelt down beside her. There was in his face an understanding look, a gentle smile, a question.

In the road some of the soldiers talked among themselves; others had seated themselves above the road. Several stood looking down at their leader and Joanna.

"Are you alone? Why did you try to run? Have you been left behind by some pilgrims going to the festival in Jerusalem?"

All the questions ran together so that Joanna didn't get a chance to answer. The Roman picked up her bread from where it had fallen when she had tried to crawl away and passed it to her. She did a strange thing; she drew her withered hand from under her robe to take the bread. Her face flushed, but the expression on the stranger's face did not change.

"Where is your staff?" he asked, looking about and pretending not to see the vexed look that flashed in the girl's eyes.

Would she tell him she didn't use one because it made her look too crippled? His dark eyes, like deep wells with sunlight reflected in them, missed nothing.

Joanna was questioning too, but silently. She studied the weathered wrinkles that lined his temples and ran together at the corners of his eyes. Some gray hair mixed with the dark curls that his helmet had pressed against his forehead. He was as tanned as the leather of his corselet. *About my father's age,* she thought. *Could Mother be wrong? Did they molest women on the road, sometimes carry them away as slaves?*

But they had killed her father. She would not say that she was from Bethel and was looking for stray sheep.

"We'll give you a Roman soldier's staff," he said and smiled. "Which way are you going on the road?"

Would she tell him that her mother was always pestering her to walk with a staff? He seemed to read her mind.

"My young soldiers will not ease their marching with a staff. They laugh at us old veterans. See the men of my company still standing and milling around like harnessed chariot horses, eager to run. They are the young; the old soldiers have fallen out to rest. We've marched most of the night; the pace is faster then, and the dust, with the dew upon it, doesn't rise to stifle us."

Why was he telling her all this?

"I have a daughter at home about your age. She, too, is beautiful and proud." Now he ceased his questions and rambling talk.

The silence embarrassed Joanna. "I'm on my way to Jerusalem," she said.

"For the Pass-day festival, or whatever your people call it?"

"The Passover. But I'm really going for something else."

"We're going there, too, to camp outside the city at a

village called Anathoth—to be on hand if rioting breaks out.

"Riots always break out when crowds gather. But the Temple people don't want soldiers in the city at festival time. So our governor, his Excellency, Pontius Pilate, humors them.

"It's hard to keep the peace among your people. They must be expecting trouble. This is the first time we've been ordered; and there already are soldiers hidden from the public within the walled grounds of Antonia, the fortress. But you started to tell me why you were going there."

"I'm going to find a man called Jesus; he heals people. I have faith that he can heal me. A friend went to inquire of him in Galilee, to see if I might go to him. But he had gone to Jerusalem."

"If you find him, I know he will make you well. You will go with us. Anathoth is only a short walk from Jerusalem." And as he was speaking he took her by the hand and began to lead her. As he went he called, "Marius, Marius."

A soldier rose from where he sat and came forward. "Yes, Petronius?"

"Spread the provisions from the litter of Phidon, the Greek, and the Macedonian slave to the other carriers. We must make room for the child to ride."

Joanna choked; her throat throbbed with a lump that hampered her breathing. She held back tears that blinded her. Benjamin had told about a Roman centurion named Petronius or Caspius whose friend or servant the Man from Nazareth had healed without even going to lay hands on him. Surely this man was the

same Petronius. The other soldier had called him Petronius. He himself had said, "I know he will make you
well." He must be the one Benjamin had heard about.
Had his expression changed when she told him she was
going to find a man named Jesus, who healed people?
She thought it had—a soft but different brightness, an
understanding.

Chapter Eight

Joanna walked along the column of soldiers, feeling almost weightless. Petronius' firm grasp at her elbow lessened her limp. There were no stares of surprise, no nervous, ill-born signs of laughter from the soldiers. Those who had seated themselves to rest rose as the centurion passed; those leaning on their staffs straightened. Joanna noticed that some were young like Benjamin; some had more gray about their brows than Petronius.

At the end of the column a soldier, wearing the same trimmings on his corselet as Petronius, was directing the removal of wine and grain skins from a litter and distributing them among other carriers. *This,* she thought, *must be Marius.* Petronius spoke to him. "We will carry this child to Anathoth. She is on her way to Jerusalem. She's heard that Jesus of Nazareth is there, and she's going to see him."

Marius smiled down and said, "The litter can be adjusted for reclining or sitting. Which would you like?"

"Show her what we mean, Phidon." Petronius spoke

to a man much older than he, wearing a short leather tunic totally unlike the soldiers' corselets. He lifted the litter's mat at one end and set a brace. The result resembled a sleeping mat propped up.

"That's if you wish to ride sitting," Marius said. "If you wish it changed, Phidon will adjust it for your comfort."

Marius, like Petronius, trained to observe with an eagle's eye acuteness, did not pause to let the girl answer. In her dark eyes that held a soft and shy expression of thanks, there was also the alert look of a young doe, ready to flee at the snap of a twig. She had an alertness born of fear. Marius had seen it.

"Phidon would much rather carry you than thrice your weight in less precious goods. He is a poet, too, and might recite or burst into song along the way. Right, Phidon?" Marius slapped the old man lightly on the shoulder as he spoke.

"Where is your partner, the Macedonian? Does he keep the pace and the cadence you set to please you?" Petronius asked.

"Yes, he is strong and does not talk my breath away as that Lydian, Axus, did." Phidon now called, "Alexander" in the direction of a small circle standing apart from the soldiers. The men in the circle were dressed like Phidon, in short leather tunics without metal plates and sandals without sole nails.

At the sound of his name, a young man, darker than the others, came from the circle. Without a word, he took up a position between the front handles of the litter. The clouded intensity of his dark face brightened into a smile in Joanna's direction.

"This is Alexander, my partner." Phidon spoke with a dignity fitting his age.

The young man bent his head with a slight jerk, then resumed his rigid stance in the presence of the centurions. There was a nervous agitation about him; he flexed his arms and rubbed his palms against his tunic, as impatient as a horse scarcely broken, restless in the traces. As a charioteer would calm his steed to gentleness, Phidon kept speaking. "He is named for his great king, Alexander. All the best Macedonian boys are named Alexander."

Joanna had heard her father speak of a renegade priest named Alexander who had defiled and paganized the Temple; but she had never heard of a Macedonian and did not know what it meant.

"Prepare to move! Route step," Petronius called loudly above the mumble of voices, stepping forward as he spoke.

Phidon and the young man stooped in cadence, lifted the litter about a cubit above the ground, and stood poised with bent backs. Marius, noticing Joanna's awkward hesitation, took her by the arm and motioned for her to take her place. He said quietly, "I think you are not used to being carried. You'll find it very pleasant."

Now the same noises that had awakened her, these strange confusing minutes ago, began: the trample of many feet, the thud of staffs against the earth, the rattle of metal against metal.

The column moves like sheep, she thought, *one soldier falling back to speak with friends and another moving up, calling to someone in front of him.* The talk and laughter was louder toward the front of the line. The men who walked near Phidon's litter spoke in whispered tones or not at all. Other litters, piled with skins, wide brass basins, drinking flasks, and fire pots, followed.

Joanna's thoughts were mingled light and dark; they raced in fear and slowed to questioned calm. She watched the morning sun flash on the polished metal plates; she studied the thick brown necks, the packs that covered broad shoulders and swayed only slightly as the soldiers walked.

Surrounded! A terrible loneliness possessed her. She was no longer a part of the road. Yesterday, with Josiah and Hannah, the road had been a bright thread of hope and its direction sure. How much better was the warmth of Barak and the softness of little Sarah's head against her. Though the sun was already up the sky, a chill shook her whole body. She missed the sound of her own footfall.

The centurion, Petronius, had not asked her if she would like to ride. Even though he had not ordered her with his booming voice to "Prepare to march! Route step," he had ordered her. "You will go with us."

All had been questions—he hadn't waited for her to answer. She was suddenly sick, sick to be back home with her mother and Martha. The swing of the litter to the step of the slaves stirred her insides. Crippled slaves were useful; they sat all day in the dust and pounded grain, turning clay at a potter's wheel. She might yet be sold.

The town they were passing must be Bethel. She should have said she was from Bethel. The column seemed to be moving faster now. Dust rose under the tramping feet. It choked her; she coughed. The slaves were used to the dust. She would escape! They would halt to rest. She would speak quietly to the old slave: "Excuse me, but I must turn aside for a moment." She would go into the bushes. And out of sight she would run.

Phidon had heard her cough. He said to the lead slave, "Let's veer to the right, Alexander, and walk out of the stream of dust."

At the edge of the road the dust was not nearly as bad. "You could pass word to the front, Phidon, and Petronius would let us carry forward."

"Ha, ha," Phidon laughed. "I am too long a slave to be so unwise. A slave does not make requests of his master."

"But you stand well with him. I remember how happy you were when he promised you that you would be the pedagogue for his children. And he always calls you to his campfire at night. What does he talk about?"

"He doesn't talk. He asks me to recite poetry I learned long ago as a boy. His favorite poets are Homer and Sophocles. He never tires of hearing Hector's farewell to his wife before he went to battle or old Priam begging Achilles for Hector's body when he was slain."

"Then with all your learning, he didn't choose you to teach his children?"

"It was old Nicandor. He had shrunk away to the shadow of a man . . ."

"Was he the pedagogue?"

"Right well he was. Servant, nurse, and teacher,

from the birth of Petronius' first child. His fingers gone stiff, he could no longer hold the stylus. His mind wandered; he called orders to his phalanx, for he had been a soldier. He grew too weak to rise from his pallet."

"And you inquired every day, 'Is old Nicandor dead?' "

"You know, Alexander, long ago a wise one of my people, named Demosthenes, said you Macedonians were barbarians—a nation of horse traders, dwelling in wattled huts and caves. He was right! You are a barbarian."

"I'm sorry, Phidon. I was only joking."

The two walked in silence now. The young slave seemed to quicken his pace. Joanna felt the uneven jerking of the broken cadence. She heard the old man's breathing. If he stumbled, she would fall. There would be loud laughter from the soldiers.

From somewhere along the column an order sounded. "Halt! Half fatigue."

The column shuffled to a halt. "That means a short rest without unbuckling packs," Phidon said to her, "but we can put the litter down and let you stretch a bit."

When the litter was on the ground, Phidon took her by the hand and helped her up. The young slave took his waterskin from where it hung about his neck and walked toward one of the litters. A soldier yelled to him, "Back, boy! You know there is no ration except at full fatigue."

Alexander returned and sat down by Phidon. The soldiers squatted in little circles, leaning against their packs. Petronius and Marius walked among them. Petronius came to where Joanna had taken a few steps aside, stamping her twisted foot to get the numbness out.

"Do you have someone in Jerusalem to care for you?" he asked.

"Yes, my mother's cousin." And other words formed—*You know the Man from Nazareth, Jesus. He healed your servant.* But Petronius had turned away and was walking among the soldiers. She didn't need to ask, anyway. It was the old man Phidon had talked about.

Phidon and Alexander were talking. The old man's eyes were afire with brightness; a questioning look, his lip sagging in unbelief, possessed Alexander's face. *Phidon has finished his story,* Joanna said to herself. She walked back to the litter. The look on her face was like that of old Phidon.

"Prepare to march! Route step." The soldiers stirred.

"We'll be in Anathoth before the sun is down," Joanna heard a soldier say.

"And never in Jerusalem, I hope," one added. "That's Pilate's hornet's nest, and he can keep it. I was there when the Jews wrecked the aqueduct; they fought like fanatics and died without a whimper. It was a bloody mess."

"Don't let Petronius ever hear you talk that way."

"Why? He wasn't there. I went up from Caesarea in Gallio's cohort."

"Not that—it's your reference to the mission, 'the emperor's mission.' That's what Petronius calls every bloody mess. He is a strange man, Petronius."

"Whatever he calls it, I say it was a bloody, bloody mess—a massacre."

"You haven't been in our cohort long. You will learn. To Petronius, old, senile, and corrupt Tiberius is 'his Highness, the Emperor'; our weak and venal Pilate is 'his Excellency, the Governor.' When he speaks to us in assembly he always says, 'I am authorized to say' or 'I am under orders'—never 'Now listen, soldiers, we . . .'

"Yet, with all that, he is a most considerate man. Before you came into the cohort, for example, he had us haul stones for nine days to help the gray-bearded priests in some little town north of the barracks build a temple; they call it a synagogue. We laughed among ourselves, knowing that if a riot broke out in that town and Petronius were ordered to quell it, there wouldn't be one stone left standing."

The column was moving now; the clank of metal and the tramp of many feet drowned out the soldier's voices. Phidon and Alexander talked as though neither had ever spoken a harsh word to the other. It was as though other persons, some inner selves, hidden and from deep within them, were speaking—not two doomed, iron-muscled men of earth, bound forever to move like yoked oxen.

Joanna listened. The upper hills with the low scrub, mottled green and brown, reminded Phidon of his island home of Paros, he said. He remembered hills running down to the bluest sea in the whole world and the path up the hill that led to the house of Formio, his teacher. He would say his lessons as he walked up the path. Here and there was a terrace, holding earth enough to keep a vine or olive tree alive. Olive trees, aged and gray, had grown tired and bent, yet never died.

A calm tenderness seemed to fill the young slave Alexander when he spoke. A small green swale far away between the hills below the road reminded him of the meadows of Macedonia. He called them glades. But in Macedonia, he said, great forests hemmed the fields.

"Ah, yes, Phidon, I'm a horse trader, too. One day I'll buy my freedom, and I'll have a field in Macedonia. I'll own a wild stallion tossing his silver mane as he gallops unbridled, his tail arched, his nostrils wide, showing off for my docile mares, switching their sleek flanks with their tails in the cool shade at the field's edge."

Their talk brought a deep solemnity to Joanna as she listened—a reverence, a hurt, an infinite, calm tenderness. She, too, would be free. And she would love the climb to the high pasture above the village of Sela. She would outrun the flock and never tire, sit on the topmost rock, listen to the hum of bees in the scrub, and come home at twilight rejoicing.

The column rested twice under the burning sun. The shoulders of the soldiers' corselets darkened with sweat.

When they rested, Joanna turned in a circle to hide her limp. Pink saffron and anemones bloomed among the stones and colored the smoother slopes. The sun had scarcely bent toward the west when the column circled the walls of a village and halted.

"This must be Anathoth," Phidon said.

"Ask Petronius to let us carry the girl to the city; then you can return and I can flee." Alexander said with a laugh.

"But you have no horse to carry you to Macedonia. Never! This is better than the mines of Thrace. That's where you'd end up."

Petronius came with a small waterskin. "This will help some," he said as he gave it to her. "It's only a few stadia. Go into the city by the Fish Gate, past the valley of the cheesemakers, and you'll be there before the sun is down. I wish we could help you on. But we have to camp here."

He walked with her past the soldiers. Phidon had said, "Bless you, my child." Alexander had said, "You brought us luck; you were only half a load. Luck go with you." Joanna formed some words but could not speak them.

A few paces past the soldiers, now spreading out and unbuckling their packs, Petronius stopped. "When you find the Man from Nazareth, tell him a Roman centurion named Petronius helped you on the way."

He turned and walked back to his men. Joanna set her broken but certain steps toward Jerusalem.

Chapter Nine

The sun was still an hour above the Judean hills when Joanna came in sight of the city. Her confidence wavered; there would be so many people. She remembered her father saying "Hold on to my tunic" as they had made their way through the crowds.

She wondered if she would pass the ruins of the tower near where they said he had died. She had been sure she could find the house of Rebecca Mark. Now she wondered. She could ask a watchman; there would be a watchman, for the gates would be left open during the time of celebration. So many people came and went.

She would not go in by the Fish Gate, as Petronius had said. The biggest crowds would be there, near the Temple. There would still be daylight enough. She would follow the road around the wall and go in by the Dung Gate. That way she would not get confused; Rebecca Mark's house was in the Street of the Dung Gate.

The clop-clop-clop of her wooden sandal was more pronounced now; the road was packed hard by many feet. She wondered if her mother would ever lose her bitterness against the city and if they would come again together as they had before her father died.

She remembered the light in her father's eyes when they came in sight of the city. He would stop and sing:

> Our feet shall stand within [your] gates, O
> Jerusalem.
>   Jerusalem
> . . . .
> to which the tribes go up,
>   the tribes of the Lord,
> . . . .
>   to give thanks to the name of the Lord.
> . . . .
> Pray for the peace of Jerusalem!
>   "May they prosper who love you!
> Peace be within your walls,
>   and security within your towers!"
>   (Ps. 122:2,4,6–7)

She took the road that turned left before the Fish Gate. The hill of the city and the wall shut out the lowering sun. This had to be the right road. There were no people here; they would be already gathered for the feast. Threads of smoke curled up from their camps in the valley and out as far as the Mount of Olives. She wondered where Josiah and Hannah were among them.

At last she came to a landmark which she recognized—the tomb of Absalom. Now she knew where she was; she sat down to rest at the steps that led to the ruins of the tower above. Her father had always stopped here and told the family the story of David's love for Absalom. Once, when she was six or seven and really understood the story for the first time, she had burst into tears. Her father had lifted her up to sit above him on one of the great hewn stones.

The Dung Gate could not be far. She remembered it as being the next gate after Absalom's tomb.

She had rested longer than she should have; suddenly she was very tired. A purple haze began to creep across the Kidron Valley.

If Jesus were camping outside the city, how would I ever find him? So many people! There were hundreds of threads of smoke from campfires. Faint sounds of singing drifted across the valley. The softness of twilight's sounds were broken only by the occasional far-off bray of a donkey tethered at some camp and the bark of a scavenger dog, assembling the pack for the night's raid.

The road ran very close to the city wall now; the clop of her wooden sandal echoed off the wall. It sounded as if someone were walking behind her, mocking her. She smiled; she had even been silly enough to look back.

The watchman at the gate might have heard. Somebody would know! She would find him!

By the time Joanna neared the Dung Gate, light-specks of the campfires across the valley and far up the slope of the Mount of Olives were beginning to dot the land. *Being late will favor me,* she thought. *I can slip past the gate in the shadows; and the beggars and lepers won't beg, pleadingly at first, and then jeer and mock.* They had at Sela once when she was with her mother, and Judith had had no alms to give.

A low fire burned at the gate. "Strange!" Joanna whispered as she paused in the dark beyond the faint circle of light and studied the one figure squatting in the fire's light. "They're all gone. Going in will be easy. This is the watchman."

Then a beautiful thought came to her. *Maybe the Man from Nazareth passed this way and healed them all. But what about the beggars?*

Just then she heard footsteps from the other direction and the peck-peck of a staff against the earth. The kneeling figure rose and stirred the fire.

An old man was revealed by its light. He was not walking with his cane; he held it straight out, tapping the wall. He was past the end of the wall and feeling the air with his stick before the watchman spoke.

"You're at the gate, old man. Move to the left or you'll walk into my fire." Joanna moved a few steps closer, careful to stay in the shadow of the wall.

"Move to the left, old man," the watchman repeated. His voice was hard and demanding. He punched the fire again. It lighted a hard, pockmarked face.

"Is this the Dung Gate?" the old man asked as he obeyed the watchman's orders, feeling the ground with his staff in a half circle in front of him.

"It is," the watchman answered. He repeated, "It is."

"It's open for the festival?" the old man spoke quietly.

"Yes, it's open for the hubbub. That's what it is, a hubbub." And he repeated the same words over again.

The old man seemed puzzled, Joanna thought, from the long silence, and he hesitated. When he did speak he did so in the same soft, hesitating manner.

"I come from across the Jordan, the village of Bethharam, in Perea."

"They come from everywhere," the watchman growled. He squatted down and leaned against the wall.

Joanna thought she might step out and lead the old man up to the fire. But he moved forward himself, firmed his staff against the ground, and leaned upon it. The fire's light picked up the white film of his sightless eyes.

"I come for a special purpose; I do not like the crowds," he said, half apologetically.

"You'll likely be trampled by them, too, in the city." The watchman showed his disgust by punching at the fire. And he repeated, "In the city." Joanna wondered if repeating everything was a habit or whether doing so made him feel his authority more. His voice reminded her of the cruel man on the road who had kicked dust into his wife's face.

"I must go in, anyway." The blind man was not going to be quieted by the watchman's rudeness. He would tell his story.

"I must find the healer from the north country. His name is Jesus, I was told. He is in the city. Have you heard of him?"

"I've heard enough! He's here and causing trouble; he's a rioter. I'm in the Temple guard, you know. This isn't my regular job. We only keep the gates when trouble is expected—mobs and things like that.

"He's got a motley mob with him, too. He has street urchins, troublemakers from the north—a hothead they call Simon Peter—and every beggar and cripple who can push his way through a crowd. Right in the Temple yard they break the law. The street urchins yell 'Hosanna, Hosanna' right in the Temple. And when the priests asked them to leave, this Jesus spoke up and said, 'Why, haven't you heard—don't you know that out of the mouths of children comes perfect praise?' And they kept yelling. The people who wanted to buy sacrifices in the Temple forecourt couldn't move for the crowd of beggars and the maimed.

"But that wasn't the worst. This rioter made a shambles of the forecourt. He upset the tables of the money changers. He opened the cages and let the doves loose; he opened the pens and released the lambs. Then he stood in front of the priests and said they'd turned a house of prayer into a den of robbers. Street waifs chased lambs all over the place. They must have carried off half a hundred. The mob was so big that Caiaphas, the high priest, held us off. Too many innocent people would be trampled. It was the worst riot I've seen since Pilate took the Temple treasury to build the aqueduct.

"As I said, I'm in the Temple guard." This time he repeated twice.

Standing so long had numbed Joanna's crippled foot. She stepped to one side. Her wooden sandal tapped against a stone.

"Who's out there? Somebody with you?" the watchman questioned, rising with his fire poker in his hand.

Joanna moved out into the light. "A girl! Another cripple. You looking for this Jesus, too? They all are."

The blind man turned and nodded in the direction of

Joanna's step. "Have you come far?" he asked. Then without waiting for an answer, he turned toward the watchman. "May I rest a minute by your fire? I walked from Bethharam to Jericho yesterday, and all the way from Jericho today."

"Sit if you will! The girl will gather dung and bundles of sticks if the fire burns down."

"I'm only passing on my way to my cousin's house in the Street of the Dung Gate. It is a lodging house; her name is Rebecca Mark. I haven't been here for several years, but I think I can find it." She ran her words together, and her fear of the watchman showed.

The blind man noticed and spoke softly. "If it's a lodging house, you'll have no trouble. There wouldn't be more than one or two on one street."

"It's the only house in the street with an upper room," the watchman growled. "You can miss it, though, if you don't watch; it's built into the hill. It is not far. Old Dame Mark is the only woman in all Jerusalem, I guess, who makes her manservant carry water. He passes here every day. It's women who should go to the well."

Joanna felt less afraid. Since the hard-faced man had told her where Rebecca's house was, he would not detain her. She stepped toward the open gate. Then she stopped—the blind man had started to speak again.

"I only heard about him two days ago; that's why I had to hurry so. Child, I hear your halted steps. Forgive me. You must be looking for him, too."

"I am. I, too, have heard of him."

"Did you hear what he did in Jericho?"

"No, not in Jericho."

The watchman closed his eyes and heaved a loud sigh. He sat down and closed his eyes as if bored by it all. His actions did not disturb the blind man.

"Sit, my child," he said. "Give me your hand. Your cousin's house is near by."

Now he spoke even more quietly, as if to respect the watchman's desire to doze. "In Jericho four days ago, or five—I only heard it two days ago—the healer, this Jesus, healed blind Bartimaeus, the son of Timaeus, the potter. I know Timaeus well; he is almost my age. I've dug clay for him in Bethharam. We have good clay in Bethharam, not silty like the valley clay. Bartimaeus used to knead clay for his father. He never wanted to learn to mold; he was too impatient."

Joanna was getting restless. She would rise and slip away if the old man continued his rambling.

"It was four or five days ago. Bartimaeus heard that this Jesus was passing through on his way up to Jerusalem. He got Shim, a camel driver, the one who told me all about it, to lead him out on the road by the gate of the Jerusalem road.

"Jesus was in a pilgrimage of a dozen or more people. So when Bartimaeus heard them coming, he began to yell to be sure he'd be heard. 'Jesus of Nazareth! Jesus! Jesus! have mercy on me' he called, as loud as he could yell. Young and fretful, Bartimaeus was about twenty-five; and he'd been born blind. He had always been impatient and had always yelled at his father, Timaeus.

"It was different with me. I could see until I was about eighteen; then the world began to get hazy and gray. In about four or five years everything was night.

"But that's the difference between me and Bartimaeus; and age makes a man more patient. You see, I could sit here by the fire all night and see the flame wave in the breeze, die down, and flare up; I remember watching it as a boy. But Bartimaeus had never seen; he never had a chance to fill up his mind with sights to remember.

"Anyway, the people in Jesus' party thought Bartimaeus' yelling was a little too brash and impatient. Two of them came forward and ordered him to shut up.

"They didn't know Bartimaeus. Then he yelled louder, Shim said, and jumped up, throwing off his robe like he wanted to fight.

"Jesus came up abreast of him and asked him what he would like for him to do for him. Then Bartimaeus spoke with a civil tongue in his mouth for the first time: 'Master, let me receive my sight!' His head was bowed, and all his bluster was gone.

"Shim was confused about what happened next. Some said Jesus stepped forward and touched Bartimaeus. Some thought he didn't—just stood facing Bartimaeus and said, 'Receive your sight; your faith has made you whole.'

"And here's tough Bartimaeus, kneeling in the road, his eyes open, crying like a baby. Then Jesus took him by the hand, made him get up, and said, 'Now you can go on your way.'

"And Bartimaeus said, 'Lord, I want to follow you.'

"Shim said there were others from Jericho, too, who joined the pilgrimage after that. I think Timaeus must have come up, too; I stopped at his clay yard and called, but everything was quiet.

"Once I said to Timaeus, 'Timaeus, you must give the boy a memory of the earth he walks. You must describe the sun and the moon and the stars, the white almond blossoms and their season, the barley fields and the green land.'

"You know what he said to me? He said, 'Jethro, Jethro,' turning his potter's wheel faster. I could hear its hum. 'How? How? God didn't even put enough words into the mouth of Moses.' "

Joanna's impatience, like Bartimaeus', was gone now. She studied the milky white film of the old man's eyes.

"If I can find Timaeus and Bartimaeus, they'll help me find the healer. I would know Bartimaeus' voice in any crowd. Your cousin will help you find him.

"I'll just stay here by the gate and go into the city in the morning. I don't have to hurry. My father taught me as a boy not to hurry. He used to be always saying, 'Hark.' And he would stand in the field and scan the sky. The distant call of the cranes, dark specks high against the sky, would come down to us. He was always saying, 'Lift up your eyes; listen; behold; look; wait; watch.' He used to forget and say it even after I was blind. I wanted to get where we were going when I was young and could see. Then, when I couldn't see, I knew his wisdom. He gave me my memory of the earth. When I smell the fields and the seasons, I can see them.

"You must go now, my child." He spoke with a whisper. "The fire is dying down; and if the watchman wakes, he might make you gather sticks for it."

The feeling of aloneness, the thought of not finding the Man from Nazareth among so many people, had left her as she sat listening to the blind man. Now that she was about to leave, it came back to her.

The watchman stirred and began to mumble something. She had been going to ask the old man if he thought that near the Temple would be the best place to find Jesus tomorrow; but now she squeezed his hand in hers without a word. He turned his sightless eyes up to her; his lips broadened with a smile, but were silent. She turned and slipped as silently into the dark street.

The mumbling of the watchman rose to a mingled snarl and growl. She listened but could not make out his words. A cloud of sparks rose from the dim red glow of the fire, now burned down to a bed of smoldering embers. Perhaps he was cursing her for having slipped away and his having missed making her search for sticks. Maybe he was repeating his talk of "that rioter" to hear the sound of his own voice; he repeated everything. Or perhaps he was just railing upon the old man without any cause.

Except for the watchman's railing, the night was still. No one moved in the street. In the houses a child would by now have asked of his father, "Why is this night different from other nights?" And the story of how Moses led the people to freedom from Pharaoh's slavery would be told. She would be too late for this tale at Rebecca Mark's house; but they would still be singing the psalms. If she got to Rebecca's house and they were still singing, she would not interrupt them. She would wait outside. If she went in, there would be too much commotion; they did not know that she was coming.

She had grown taller; they might not recognize her.

Yes, they would know her.

Martha and her mother would be at Benjamin's house for the feast. Martha and Benjamin would be saying, 'Joanna is celebrating the feast with your cousin. She is probably there long before now.'

But all the time Joanna's thoughts kept returning to Jethro, the blind man. After the surprise at her coming, Rebecca Mark would make her sit and eat, and they would pass the wine and sing more psalms for her. Jethro was a gentle man of faith. He was here at the gate of the city at Passover time. Perhaps he had not been here the whole time since he was blind. Why had she not taken him by the hand and led him along the dark street with her to Rebecca's house?

This was the night of all nights of the year most important for the stranger to be comforted. She would go back and get him. She would do for him as Josiah and Hannah and Petronius had done for her. If he had said, "Your cousin has a lodging house; perhaps I could lodge there tonight," she would have thought, *Of course*. She would go back and bring him. Besides, the moon was not up; and she was having a hard time seeing the dark walls of the houses to find the one that would be higher than the others because of its upper room.

She had retraced her steps only a little way when she heard the sound of footsteps behind her. She crouched by the steps that led up to a rooftop. From inside the house there came a quiet voice. *The prayers for deliverance,* she thought.

Several figures passed, almost within arm's reach. They walked slowly and in silence. She was about to continue when she heard more footsteps. This time the feet were running. The blur in the darkness seemed smaller than those just passed; the lightness of the steps seemed to be those of a boy. She listened. No one came after the runner.

She made her way back to the Dung Gate, dreading to come again within the sound of the pock-faced watchman's snarling voice but determined to lead the blind man, who too was seeking the Man from Nazareth, to a place of lodging for the night. She need not have dreaded the watchman. He sat hunched with his back to the wall, his snoring almost as coarse as his voice. The fire was so low that the circle of light where she had sat with Jethro was now dark. She peered into the dark; the blind man was not there.

Not letting her wooden sandal clop once against the earth, she went through the gate. Had the watchman driven him away? She went a distance along the wall on either side of the gate. She listened for the tap of his cane against the wall. Perhaps he had found the warmth of the watchman's fire too costly a price to pay for his unpleasantness and had sought a quiet place outside the walls. She called. No answer. Perhaps the people who passed in the street had been pilgrims who had celebrated the feast in the city with friends. They had pitied him and taken him to their camp.

She slipped noiselessly back through the gate. The moon was just above the houses now. She would have no trouble finding her way. She would be so glad for rest.

She was also confused. The three days on the road, despite the death of the pet lamb, Rachel, and the comments of the cruel man who had said, "These beggars and cripples shouldn't clutter up the city at Passover time," had filled her with more and more hope as she neared the holy city. Even though the thought of "so many people" had disturbed her, she had imagined all of them trying to get near the wonderful Man from Nazareth, to hear him teach, to tell his beautiful stories to others—ones like Benjamin had told her. And whoever was near him would go home and tell others that he had seen the miracle worker.

But the watchman's cruel talk would not go away—"rioter, troublemaker, faker." His words mixed fear with her hope. Jethro, the blind man, believed; but he had vanished in the night. Suppose Rebecca and Rhoda and John Mark didn't believe? Suppose their talk was like that of the watchman?

Well, she had come far into the street; she would soon know. The houses she was passing were built against the hill that rose sharply behind them. Rebecca Mark's house couldn't be far. The watchman had said Rebecca's lodging house was built into the hill.

Chapter Ten

In the moonlight Joanna stood studying the house that rose taller than those around it. She was about to move to the door and knock when it opened. A woman with a lamp in her hand moved to the foot of the steps that led up to the room above and called, "John—John Mark."

No answer. The woman held the lamp above her head and made her way up the steps. She stood at the door, listening. She knocked—the door did not open. She pulled the latchstring and pushed the door ajar. "I didn't hear anyone go out," she said aloud. "I told him to bring down the bowls if the men were finished." The woman closed the door and made her way down the steps.

Joanna coughed. She did not want to frighten Rebecca. Ever since her father died, her mother had always scolded when someone approached in the dark without calling out.

"Is that you, John?" The woman stopped.

"It is Joanna, your cousin Judith's girl."

"And Judith and Martha?"

"No, I am alone."

"Alone, child! Alone!"

Rebecca held the lamp up to Joanna's face. "It is; it is!" she cried as she stooped and put the lamp on the ground. She took Joanna in her arms and kissed her on both cheeks, which now were streaming with tears.

"I came alone, against Mother's will." Joanna tried to control her voice. It would not rise above a broken whisper. "We heard of Jesus, the great healer—that he had left Galilee and come here."

Rebecca held the trembling girl close against her warm body. "I know that he will heal me if I can find him."

"You will find him, child. The Lord has sent you— signs and wonders. You must rest now and eat."

Rebecca was almost carrying her as they entered the house. She called as she went, "Rhoda, Rhoda! Bring water and oil to wash our wayfarer's feet. Someone all the way from the north country—Joanna—alone, the dear child, Joanna."

Through the closed door of the house in the Street of the Dung Gate, excited voices overrunning each other with questions drifted out upon the quiet night. After Rebecca had heard Joanna's story and asked about Judith and the friends in Sela, Rhoda took the dish from which Joanna had eaten and washed it. Rebecca sat down by Joanna, took her by the hand, and began her story.

"You will find the great healer, my dear. This will surprise you. But he was in this house this very night.

"We have had a strange day and a strange week. I wonder where John Mark could be? I sent him to the upper room to bring down the bowls if the men were finished. They had all vanished, and John Mark was with them.

"I'm getting ahead of my story. I must go back. Early this morning when Alphaeus came from the well, two men followed him. When John Mark saw them he said he had seen them in the Temple with Jesus, the teacher. Oh! I forgot to say that it all started earlier in the week when Jesus drove the money changers out of the Temple court. John Mark was there, and he's been going back every day this week looking for more excitement. But the teacher has only been talking and healing the sick.

"My boy is taken with him. That's where he is now, I guess. They're camping somewhere outside the city.

"The two said they needed a room big enough for their Master and twelve followers to celebrate the Passover feast. Could I rent them the room over the house? John Mark whispered to me not to charge. But before I had a chance to think, he blurted out that they could use it free. The men then went away, and my boy went with them. Then at sundown or a little after, Jesus, John Mark, and the followers came. There were, as the men had said, twelve of the followers."

Joanna could contain herself no longer. "What did he look like? Did Rhoda see him, too? If I had only been here."

"He was younger than I thought he would be, from what John Mark had said; but he had deep, sorrowful eyes that made him look older than his years."

Rhoda had seen him. "What did he . . . ?" But Joanna did not get a chance to finish. Rebecca inter-

rupted. "John Mark served them—foot water, wine, bitter herbs—up and down, up and down. Up listening and serving mostly, except that when he came for more bread I asked why there was no singing of the psalms. He said they were arguing about something.

"One of them left, and John Mark went out and called after him; but he was gone. I had to go out and tell the boy to stop yelling in the street. He'd disturb the neighbors. The one who left was named Judas, I think.

"That's about it. John Mark can tell you more about Jesus' teaching in the Temple. Then we made John sit at meat with us. I told him to bring down the bowls they were finished with, so we could clean them all up together. We waited and waited; then I went up, and they were all gone—John, too.

"Did I miss anything, Rhoda? John Mark has all kinds of stories about the teacher's preaching and healing and taking the sick, the street children, and the homeless right into the Temple.

"But it's late, and first thing in the morning he'll be dragging you on the run to wherever the healer is camped."

"If I had only known. They passed me in the street, and I hid by some steps that led up to a rooftop. And somebody was behind them, running." Joanna began to sob.

"That was surely that boy. Now don't you worry; you haven't missed him. You must rest now."

"I did forget one thing," Rhoda said quietly after the fire was covered and they had lain down to sleep. "His eyes were only deep and sorrowful, old-looking, when

he wasn't looking at anybody. When he was talking to
you, and he just said a few words to me—thanked me for
a cloth for the table that John forgot and I took up—then
his eyes were soft and wistful, like a child who has
stopped crying, dried his tears, and started to smile.
You know."

"Your foot—does it hurt?"

"No. I was just turning over," Joanna answered. "I
was so tired in the dark street. Now I'm not tired at all.
I didn't think I'd ever get here, I guess."

Rebecca was lying awake, listening. "Rhoda, did you
hear the door to the lodging room?"

Rhoda did not answer. She was lost in her own
thoughts. In the mingled routine and different events
of the day, it had fallen her lot to carry a tablecloth to
the upper room and to hand it to a man named Jesus,
whom her friends called Master. He had looked into
her eyes and said, "Bless you, my child." Yet he was not
of an age to speak in a fatherly way. He was not much
older than some of Rhoda's friends in the street. She
closed her eyes, remembering the look in his—without
quest or question, warm enough to melt the distance
between hearts. The thought brought instant peace
and sleep.

Rebecca turned quietly on her bed, listening for
sounds. She heard the sound of a boy's footsteps, the
sound of a robber moving with stealthy steps on the
other side of the wall. The door to the lodging room had
opened.

Would this child be disappointed after her long journey of hope? This healer, this teacher—could all the
things she had heard about him be true? "What did he

look like?" the girl had asked. That had been her first question. "What did he look like?"

The two who had come to engage the room seemed more in command; they talked more. The big one with the heavy Galilean accent seemed more forceful. Yet the boy had said, "No other rabbi ever spoke as this man does."

She had forgotten to go back and bring in the lamp where she had left it, on the step, when she took the crippled child in her arms. It had burned out of oil. She hoped John Mark wouldn't stumble over it and cause it to break. She was too tired to worry about it tonight.

Joanna was still wide awake. She felt a throbbing in her foot. She only felt it, a pulsing without pain. "He was here," she whispered to herself over and over. He had passed her in the street, he and his friends. That had been John Mark running to catch up. What if she had not gone back to get Jethro, the blind man? She would have been here in time.

That's why I couldn't find Jethro. He healed Jethro when he found him at the gate. Jethro had gone with him and his followers. Right now he would be sitting around their campfire saying, "Master, Master! Now I can see the sun and the moon and the stars, the white almond blossoms and their season, the barley fields and the green land." Yes, Jethro would say the same thing he had said to Timaeus, the potter.

What would she say to him? "Master, Master! Now I can outrun the lambs in the high pasture. I can turn back the wayward stray to the flock. I can tread in the winepress and dance at the Feast of the Tabernacles. I can walk the earth and hear its music—it will not ever again be drowned out by the clop-clop-clop of my wooden sandal."

That's what she would say. Or perhaps as, in front of Petronius, the centurion, who had been so kind to her, she would not be able to say anything because her lips trembled and her heart filled up her throat.

With thoughts of running the high pasture, waving to her mother in the fields—peace at last. Sleep came to Joanna.

Joanna awakened to the sound of soft voices. A pungent smell filled the room. Rhoda sat at her feet, stirring a small jar. "Your foot is very swollen from all your walking. This calmus-olive oil ointment will take the swelling down."

"It hardly hurts at all," Joanna answered as she sat up.

Rebecca stood in the open door. When she heard Joanna's voice she lowered her own to a whisper. It was still early morning. The open door framed a deep henna sky, clear but lacking the brightness of a cloudless dawn.

The person to whom Rebecca spoke was out of view beyond the edge of the door. Joanna picked up the fragment of a statement from the unseen speaker: "Come back here and wait." Was it the Man from Nazareth? Perhaps Rebecca and John Mark had planned a surprise. She wouldn't ask.

Was that John Mark speaking? No, he wouldn't be standing outside. He was probably asleep in the lodgers' room. When he awakened he could tell her where the Man from Nazareth was.

The penetrating warmth of the ointment soaked in and came halfway up her leg as Rhoda gently rubbed. "Ah, it is so warming. It tingles, too, and makes me feel like running."

"It will work fast. Don't worry about smelling like a calmus root. This is oil of rue." Rhoda held up another small jar. "It'll take the smell away."

"Speaking of running, I had the queerest dream last night. It was scary like one I had the first night I was on the road, but silly, too."

"You were so tired."

Rebecca now went out and closed the door behind her. Joanna was about to ask who was outside when Rhoda spoke. "What did you dream? Here," she began to rub the amber-colored rue on Joanna's ankle, "this will make the calmus smell better."

"I dreamed that I was healed and riding back home to Sela on a donkey. But it was so silly—the donkey was green. I knew exactly how it looked—pale green like lily of the valley leaves."

"Ah, that's easy. Alphaeus' father has donkeys for hire outside the city wall. We'll put a soft green coverlet on one and have John Mark take you home in triumph."

"All along the way people stopped and stared."

"And who wouldn't if they saw a green donkey, especially a pale green one?"

"They jeered and laughed and ran after me."

"Well, we are laughing now. Can you blame them? I don't see anything scary about that."

"When I got home"—now Joanna's voice became serious—"Mother said, 'Don't turn that donkey loose to graze; it'll rob the flocks of their pasture. The neighbors will complain.'

"I don't know what happened then. I don't know whether I turned it loose or not or how much time had passed. But the whole earth was brown; all the grass was eaten; and the leaves were stripped from the thornbushes and roses. And the only green thing on the earth was that light green donkey."

"Believe me, that's one a sorcerer at the Dung Gate would earn his barley cake for explaining. Your stomach must have been riled from eating too much after going hungry so long."

"All the flocks were dead and scattered on the brown hills. And every day all the people in the village came out and tried to catch the donkey. They ran through the bare thornbushes and tore their clothes and flesh. And I ran faster than anyone in the whole village, including the boys and men. And they were all yelling, 'Joanna! Joanna! Joanna will catch it.' Then I woke up."

"We'll be sure to tell Alphaeus to get a tame donkey from his father. Look! The swelling is going down already, and the redness is gone."

"What is all that talking in the street?" Joanna asked. The street had suddenly become alive with voices. Could it be that the Man from Nazareth and his followers were returning? Joanna had heard the speaker outside the door say something about "coming back" or "they'll come back."

Rhoda rose to look; but as she did the door opened, and Rebecca and John Mark stepped inside and closed it. "The beggars are returning to their place outside the gate," Rebecca said. "We can't give bread to one and not to all. They've been slipping into the city all week to find the healer; every one of them has something he wants cured."

"The Temple guards tried to drive them out the first day after Jesus came, but the crowds were too big; and they lost control." Joanna had started to rise as John Mark spoke. He came and took her by the hand. Joanna did not speak. She fingered her robe and covered her ankle.

Rebecca, wise and knowing the awkwardness that overtakes the young, spoke. "You two have grown up so much you wouldn't have known each other."

Joanna's thoughts were on other things, but she noticed that the robe John Mark was wearing was much too large for him. It almost touched the ground. "Your mother says you will take me to the Man from Nazareth so he can heal me."

A troubled faraway look, which he could not hide, came over the boy's face as Joanna continued. "Or is he coming here again? I heard you say somebody would come back and wait."

"Yes," the boy said after a moment, "probably later. There's been a big mix-up. The Temple people, the Pharisees and the scribes, have been after him all week since a ruckus in the Temple.

"And last night the Temple guards arrested him.

"I've been out all night. When I came back to let Mother know where I was, they had taken him to Pilate for questioning. I told John Boanerges, one of the followers, to tell the others that they could come back here and wait.

Chapter Eleven

Joanna would not be dissuaded. She had come against her mother's wishes. She would not stop now. Up through the streets, somewhere—but no such journey as the long trek from the hill country—she would go. She would find him now. The pleadings of Rhoda and Rebecca she scarcely heard.

"You should wait; there's still some swelling in your foot."

"John Mark knows he will be glad to come. Besides, it will be better here. Maybe he won't do any more miracles in public. His great works make the Temple people mad."

The barley bread and broth were ready. The four sat in a circle and ate.

Rhoda and Rebecca found more reasons. "The mob will be clearing out today. Only the few who can afford to stay for the days of unleavened bread will stay."

The boy and the crippled girl listened. They said nothing. Joanna had made her pronouncement.

She studied the look on John Mark's face. Would he go with her? He was older now. He wouldn't let her go

Caesar what is Caesar's, and to God what is God's.' So they couldn't accuse him of being disloyal to God or against doing what the Romans demand.

"He called the Pharisees and scribes 'hypocrites and vipers' right to their faces, in front of all the people. But they kept coming back with more questions. And they were being hypocrites. They called him 'Master.' 'Master,' they said, 'we know your wisdom comes from above. Now then tell us, which is the great and first Commandment?' This was a lawyer asking, trying to trap him.

"Jesus looked him straight in the eye and answered: 'You shall love the Lord with all your heart, and with all your soul, and with all your mind. This is the first and great commandment. And the second is like unto it: You shall love your neighbor as yourself.'

"I was thinking about that while I walked home that day. If everybody kept these commandments, that would be all the laws anybody would ever need.

"I used to yell at Alphaeus, the servant who works for Mother. I used to kick him around and be mean to him. But I'm not anymore. It's only been three days, and he hasn't noticed it yet. He still leaves when I come around.

"Stop a minute. I have to gather this robe about me. It's too big for me." The boy pulled the robe closer about his shoulders, took Joanna's hand again, and continued on the way.

"I lost mine last night and had to run home in my loincloth to get this one. I was up all night."

"But how could you lose your robe?" Joanna spoke for the first time.

"When the Temple guards first showed up to arrest him, we were going to fight. Peter and Andrew both had swords. Peter took a cut at one of them and split his ear. Then Jesus said to Peter, 'Put away your sword; don't you know that they who take up the sword shall surely perish by the sword?' Then he walked right up to the Temple guard and touched his ear; and it was healed. The Temple guards had swords and spears, but he stood right in the middle of them. And Judas and the one whose ear he touched looked more stupid than the rest."

"But who was Judas?"

"Oh, that's right. You didn't hear me telling Mother what happened. So I'll go back to the beginning.

"In the upper room there was some kind of an argument. I didn't hear it all because I was going up and down, serving the meal for Mother. Judas was one of Jesus' followers. When the argument was going on, Jesus said, 'One of you will betray me.' Then they were all saying, 'Is it I, Master?' When it came to Judas, Jesus looked at him and said, 'What you're going to do, do quickly.'

"Peter jumped up and said, 'Not I, Master. Never.' Jesus looked at him, and I thought he sort of smiled. 'Peter,' he said very quietly, 'before the cock crows at dawn you will have denied that you even know me—not once, but three times.' Then Mother called me, and I had to go to bring up something.

"On the way back up I met Judas going down the steps. When I put the dish down for them, I went out quickly and ran into the street, calling after Judas. I don't know what I thought I could do. Anyway, he was gone.

"Then Mother made me come in and eat. When I went back up to the upper room, they were gone. I ran after them, for I knew they were camping somewhere across the valley on the Mount of Olives. I caught up with them at the Dung Gate."

"Did you see an old blind man there by the watchman's fire? Did Jesus see him?"

"Yes, that's how I caught up with them. How did you know?"

"I had come that way. I talked to the old man. I hid when you passed in the dark. When they passed, too. If I had only known."

"They had been talking, I guess, for just when I got to the gate, Jesus said, 'You will receive your sight.' The old man just stood; then he began to weep. 'Master, Master. I will follow you.' And he fell down and began to kiss Jesus' feet. Jesus raised him up and said, 'No, go your way. And tell no man what has happened. Your faith has made you whole.' Then suddenly the watchman, a hard-faced man with a set sneer, jumped up and ran into the night. When I looked back the old man was standing in the gate; he hadn't moved.

"But you're sobbing."

"I know. I can't help it. I talked to the old man by the fire. His name was Jethro. I might have been there, too."

"Here, dry these tears." The boy turned his palms outward and wiped Joanna's cheeks. "We could sit by the wall and rest awhile. We'll probably have to wait outside the palace gate, anyway. You can be sure Pilate is not going to hurry his morning to accommodate the Temple people; they hate each other."

"I'm all right. Let's go on. You left off from your story at the gate."

"After that everybody walked in silence. No one said a word until he had crossed Kidron Brook and come up to the olivepresses in the grove at the foot of Mount Olive. There Jesus said, 'I need to be alone to pray. Wait here.' And he went into the garden of the olive-presses, Gethsemane.

"It wasn't long after that till the Temple guards came. Judas came with them. That part I told you. Then they tried to grab us, too. One of the guards reached for me and got hold of my robe. I ran out of it. Everybody scattered in a different direction. John Boanerges ran past me and said, 'We'll gather back at your house and wait.'

"I came back, running in my loincloth. After I waited and no one showed up, I went to the Temple court. Peter and John were there, but none of the others.

"There was a crowd of people around the fire in the courtyard. Some girl pointed to Peter and said, 'He's one of them. I saw him with him when he was preaching in the colonnade.' Peter looked at her and said, 'I never saw the man.' She repeated it twice more, and both times Peter denied he knew Jesus. Then somewhere, far away—but you could hear it even above the mumble of people talking—I heard a rooster crow. I looked across at Peter; he was wiping away tears with the back of his hand.

"All this time Jesus was somewhere inside being questioned by the high priest, Caiaphas, and his father-in-law, old Annas. They run the city and hate the Romans, but fear any uprising lest the Romans take away what power they have.

"When I looked again, Peter was gone. The doves began to coo nearby. It was daylight, and I thought I had better come home and let Mother know where I was.

"John was in a crowd outside the gate. He had seen Peter go by in a hurry, but hadn't gotten to him through the crowd; he didn't know where the others were. He had only seen Andrew to tell him to meet back at my house.

"There was a commotion in the courtyard. Guards were yelling, 'Clear the yard!' Two of them took up stations at the gate and began to talk. One asked the other what the old man, meaning Caiaphas, was going to do with the imposter who was causing riots, claiming to be the son of God and the king of the Jews all at the same time. His companion answered that Caiaphas was going to send him to Pilate sometime during the morning.

"Those Romans have a reputation for drinking and feasting all night, Pilate more than most. It'll be a while, probably. We'll go to the courtyard of Caiaphas' palace first. We'll wait at the gate, and when Jesus comes out—but what about the Temple guard? They might not let you talk to him."

"It won't make any difference." Joanna spoke with a confidence that surprised the boy. "I will look at him, and he will look at me; and I will never have to hide my withered arm and hobble upon my twisted ankle again."

The boy had really been talking to himself when he

had asked the last question. The streets were wider now, the walls more massive and foreboding. There were more people, and they all seemed to be hurrying. The grave thoughts he had whispered to his mother earlier had come back to the boy. But Joanna's confidence had so surprised him that he spoke no more aloud. None of the followers of the Master had come back. That puzzled him.

He hadn't told the girl about the hostility of the crowd who filled Caiaphas' palace yard. Where had they come from? All the days before they had cheered the Man from Nazareth, called him Teacher, and yelled "Hosanna!" Last night he had studied their faces. He couldn't tell whether they were the same people. All he knew now was that they stood grim faced and that they muttered under their breath; and when an occasional cry of "Down with him" arose, they waved their arms aloft and shouted.

The boy wearing the robe too big for him and the girl limping by his side now walked in silence. They seemed to be the only quiet people in the street. The girl held on tightly to the boy's hand; the dread of so many people around came back to her.

Once or twice she was pushed; she almost fell, moving aside quickly to avoid the human tide that seemingly moved without direction. Some glanced at the crippled girl; one or two said "Excuse me." But most paid no attention. The maimed and rejected were always with them—a part of life.

To hide her embarrassment at almost having fallen several times, she broke the silence. "We seem to be the only ones who know where we are going," she had said.

The boy did not answer.

Her voice had faltered, had been unsure. Would she be able to speak when she came face to face with the Man from Nazareth—the great healer—the teacher—the Master? No, she must do more than just look at him. She must call out. She must not let her voice tremble and quaver. What would she call him—master—teacher—healer—Jesus, Son of God? What would she say—"I believe"—"My faith has brought me to you"—or would she fall down before him and he would know her meaning?

In the distance the sun had climbed high above the towers of the fortress Antonia; it was above a hill called Golgotha, the place of the skull. In the Valley of the Cheesemakers and Kidron, over the Mount of Olives, it was burning off the last wavering strings of morning's mist.

Chapter Twelve

Soldiers stood dividing the crowd that jammed the way to Pilate's palace yard. Along the street that led to the Ephraim Gate there seemed to be more order, with soldiers lining either side at measured intervals. In their confusion and terror, Joanna and John Mark were swept along.

Women were pushed aside by men who called to each other as they ran. "Save me a place." "There's three of them." "One is Barabbas, who slit the three soldiers' throats and threw their bodies into Pilate's pool." "No! two thieves and a rioter."

"Clear the street; clear the street," the soldiers repeated. Their staccato voices were so ineffective that some prodded the crowd with the blunt end of their spears. A crowd of boys mocked them ("Clear the street; clear the street") in their high-pitched voices, panting as they raced. "Save me a place on the wall," one who could not keep up called after his friends.

A soldier touched Joanna and pulled her aside. A certain gentleness and even some kindness showed through his grim face. "Stand here," he said, "or you'll be trampled."

A woman gave John Mark a hard look for having taken a place in front of her, but she said nothing. Everyone immediately around them were women except a dark-skinned man, a foreigner by his dress, with two small boys. Several of the women held their napkins up to their faces.

A prolonged groan, broken by a shout at times, rose like a wind, increasing its howl as it came.

Joanna and John Mark's words to each other had been lost; they had no meaning. Later they would never try to recapture them.

What is Joanna saying? Whose name is this she is crying out? A woman nudges her and says, "Be quiet, child!"

An awesome procession has come into view. At its head a soldier marches erect, his sword swinging to the rhythm of his step. He studies the crowd with hard eyes. His look is grim. He does not hear a voice calling, "Petronius, Petronius!" Or, if he does hear, he does not look around.

Twelve soldiers form a wall on either side of three figures, moaned for and jeered at, as they pass a given point. Behind, a column of soldiers fills up the street. Behind the soldiers, the crowd breaks like a dam at floodcrest. A human sea follows.

Each of the three figures carries the crossbeam of the cross upon which he will be nailed—a practice to show others the consequences of crime. The figure in front holds his head up; he looks to one side and then the other, as though searching for someone—someone to whom he might speak. The two following look only at the ground, never once raising their eyes. The one in front is wearing a white robe that shows pink welts across the shoulders where blood from whiplashes is beginning to ooze through. Someone had twisted thornbush branches into a wreath and pushed it down upon his brow. The two following wear brown tunics of the street and field.

Now the foremost figure slows his step. He is looking at the women—or is it Joanna he sees? He speaks; his voice is not that of one cowed by fear and forlorn of hope. "Do not weep for me." A tender light comes to his eyes. "Weep for yourselves and for your children."

Joanna threw herself forward. She touched his robe. And when she did, he stumbled. A soldier stepped forward and pulled her back. At the same time he pointed to a dark-skinned man. "Here, you," he said, "carry this crossbeam." Did the soldier pick him out because he was standing in the crowd of women or because he stood apart?

"But I have my children," the man protested. Turning to the two little boys he said, "Follow"; then he lifted the wooden beam from the other's shoulders.

The man in the white robe did not look back. Was he remembering long ago in Galilee, by the sea, when thousands sought to hear him and a great multitude pressed upon him? Did he think of how he had turned abruptly in the crowd and said, "Who touched me? I perceive that power has gone out of me." And all at first denied; but slowly from the crowd a poor woman came trembling. Falling down before him, she said, "I knew that if I could only touch your garment I would

be healed." And he had said to her, "Daughter, your faith has made you whole. Go in peace."

Or, glancing up into the face of the dark-skinned man, now taking the crossbeam from his shoulders, did other words he had once spoken come back to him: "A prophet is not without honor save in his own country, and among his own kin"?

The soldier who had pulled Joanna back from the street pushed her a bit too hard among the cluster of women. A woman with a stern and morbid look on her face, with no napkin in her hand, gave Joanna another push, saying as she did, "You caused the poor man to stumble; you unclean wretch!"

But in all the pushing, Joanna did not fall. She did not even stumble. She would never stumble again because of her crippled foot. Her faith had made her whole.

In the Street of the Ephraim Gate, which men would rename the Street of Sorrows, *Via Dolorosa,* two great stones guarded the entrance to a rich man's garden. Between these stones the girl and the boy huddled for shelter. When the human tide had surged past, they turned the other way. "Follow me," the girl said, leading the way. And they went on in silence.

"And the blind and the lame came to him in the temple, and he healed them. But when the chief priests and the scribes saw the wonderful things that he did, and the children crying out in the temple, 'Hosanna to the Son of David!' they were indignant; and they said to him, 'Do you hear what these are saying?' And Jesus said to them, "Yes; have you never read,

'Out of the mouths of babes and sucklings thou hast brought perfect praise'?"

Matthew 21:14–16

"It is the spirit that gives life, the flesh is of no avail; the words that I have spoken to you are spirit and life."

John 6:63

"Many believed in his name when they saw the signs which he did; but Jesus did not trust himself to them, because he knew all men and needed no one to bear witness of man; for he himself knew what was in man."

John 2:23

"Seeing they may not see, and hearing they may not understand."

Luke 8:10